A Star in the Saddle

"I think you're jealous of all of us," Kathy told Linda over the phone. "You're mad because we all got parts on 'Diamond Street' and you didn't. And I think that stinks!" Kathy banged down the phone.

Slowly, Linda replaced the receiver. She sat down on the edge of the den's comfortable old sofa. Her stomach felt as if it were filled with lead.

"Honey?" Bronco asked gently. "What's the matter?"

"Oh, Bronco!" Linda ran over to hug him.

"Now, what's wrong?" Bronco asked. "You can tell your grandpa."

Linda swallowed hard to keep from crying. "I think I just lost my best friend!"

Books in The Linda Craig Adventures series:

Available from MINSTREL Books

THE LINDA CRAIG ADVENTURES #8

A STAR IN THE SADDLE

By Ann Sheldon

A MINSTREL® BOOK

PUBLISHED BY POCKET BOOKS

New York   London   Toronto   Sydney   Tokyo

A MINSTREL PAPERBACK *ORIGINAL*

A Minstrel Book published by
POCKET BOOKS, a division of Simon & Schuster Inc.
1230 Avenue of the Americas, New York, NY 10020

ISBN: 0-671-67472-2

First Minstrel Books printing July 1989

10 9 8 7 6 5 4 3 2 1

A STAR IN THE SADDLE

1 ♦♦♦♦

"Oh, Roger, it's Stephanie! She's . . . she's gone! Our little girl has run away!"

"Wow!" Linda Craig's dark eyes were wide as she turned to look at her best friend, Kathy Hamilton. "Do you think she really ran away? Or do you think those guys in the black limo kidnapped her?"

"I don't know." Kathy shook her head, her honey blond hair swirling. "All I know is, it's a terrible way to end the season. Now we have to wait until next fall to find out what *really* happened!"

It was a Monday morning in June. The girls were at Linda's house, watching a videotape of their favorite television program, "Diamond Street." Normally, they never would have missed it at its regular time, but the night before had been a special occasion— Mac's birthday party.

Mac was the foreman of Linda's grandparents' ranch, Rancho del Sol, where Linda and her brother, Bob, had lived since their parents died. With his easygoing smile and expert knowledge of horses, Mac was one of Linda's favorite people in the world. So she and Kathy had been willing to miss the last episode of "Diamond Street" for him—especially since they could watch it the next morning on the VCR.

Just then Linda's grandmother, "Doña" Rosalinda Mallory, bustled into the den. *Doña* was a Spanish title of respect—and that's what everyone called Mrs. Mallory. Linda thought it was because Doña looked so regal, with her crown of dark hair and her erect horsewoman's posture. And, of course, Doña *was* Spanish by heritage.

Doña took a checkbook out from one of the desk drawers. "It's a gorgeous day," she said. "Why aren't you girls outside, instead of cooped up in this dark old room watching TV? When I was twelve, and my summer vacation had just begun, you wouldn't catch me spending my time in front of a television."

"You didn't have a television when you were twelve," Linda reminded her grandmother.

"True." Doña laughed. "All the same, I think you girls should get out—maybe take a ride into town. I

2

hear some Hollywood people are here—filming a movie, I suppose."

"Hey, that's right!" Linda scrambled to her feet. "What time is it?"

Kathy looked at her watch. "Almost eleven," she said, jumping up. "And we're supposed to be at Amy and Marni's house by noon. Doña, there might be extra parts in this film. We're going to find out if maybe we can be in it!"

"How exciting!" Doña said.

"Well, we'd better get going," Linda said. She gave her grandmother a peck on the cheek. "Wish us luck."

"I certainly do," Doña called after them as they hurried to the door.

Outside, Linda and Kathy crossed the broad sweep of lawn in front of the ranch house. Linda paused to take a deep breath of the sun-warmed Southern California air. "Doña was right," she said. "It was a little cloudy early this morning, but now it *is* a gorgeous day."

"Mmm," Kathy agreed. "The air smells kind of smoky. Like it does in the fall—know what I mean?"

"Yup. But it's not fall—it's summer vacation." Linda grinned. "Hollywood, here we come!" She ran to the corral, Kathy right behind her.

3

At the corral gate, Linda put her fingers to her lips and gave a shrill whistle. Instantly there was an answering nicker.

Then a beautiful palomino mare came trotting over to them from the salt lick. Her golden hide gleamed in the sun, and her large brown eyes were alight with intelligence. With another nicker, she reached her head over the gate and nuzzled Linda's shoulder.

"Good morning, Amber," Linda said, stroking her horse's neck. "Ready for some fun today, girl?"

As if in answer, Amber bobbed her head up and down and stamped her front hoof.

Kathy laughed. "Amber, you really are something," she said admiringly. "I'll bet you could teach Patches a thing or two. Not that I don't love him just the way he is," she added.

Patches was Kathy's brown-and-white pinto. He was an easygoing horse, who would rather eat and sleep than gallop around. Now he moseyed over to where Amber and the girls were. Fluttering his lips in a breathy horse-sigh, he gave Kathy a resigned look. He seemed to be saying, "Are we going to go out *again?*"

"Yes, Patches, it's time," Kathy told him. "Now, stop looking so unhappy about it."

4

Amber nudged Patches with her head and gave a little whinny. "Look, Amber's telling him to cheer up," Linda commented, grinning.

She unlatched the gate, and the two girls led their horses over to the barn. As they entered the cool, dark, hay-scented building, a kitten and a few chickens scrambled to get out of their way.

They got their saddles and bridles from the tack room. Linda pulled her new saddle blanket down from the rack. Her grandfather had brought it from Mexico for her a couple of weeks before. It was made of thick, soft white cotton, with bright blue stripes. Linda thought it looked great with Amber's golden coat and white mane and tail.

Setting the tack down on the railing, Linda unbuckled Amber's rope halter and slipped it off. She picked up the bridle, cupping the metal bit in her hands for a moment to warm it up. "I know you hate cold bits," she murmured as she slid the metal between Amber's teeth. Then she adjusted the headstall over Amber's ears.

Next to them, Kathy poked Patches in the ribs. "Come on, stop holding your breath, horse," she coaxed. "You don't want this girth to be so loose that I fall off, do you?"

Linda chuckled. "Maybe that's exactly what he does want," she suggested. "That way he won't have to go anywhere."

The girls finished tacking up, mounted, and rode out of the barn and into the sunlight again. Amber tossed her head and pranced sideways, testing the breeze with her flaring nostrils. "You're raring to run, aren't you, girl?" Linda asked. The mare whinnied in response.

"Oh, go ahead," Kathy said from behind them. "Patches and I will catch up with you."

"Well . . ." Linda felt a little bit bad about leaving her friend behind, but when Amber wanted to run, there was no way Patches could keep up with her. Not many horses could, as a matter of fact. Amber galloped as if she had wings on her feet.

"Okay, we'll meet you at the road," she said, flashing a smile at Kathy. "Let's go, wonder horse!" She touched her heels to Amber's flanks, and they were off.

At first Linda kept Amber to a smooth lope, enjoying the gentle rocking motion. Then, sensing the mare's eagerness, she let Amber have her head.

As soon as Amber felt the pressure on her reins slacken, she shot forward. Linda could feel the

6

horse's powerful muscles bunch and release, as her stride ate up the ground.

Linda pulled off her cowboy hat and waved it in the air. The wind whipped at her hair, tugging long dark strands out of her single braid. "Yippee!" she shouted.

They were still going at full speed when they came to a high hedge at the edge of an open field. Linda put her tongue between her teeth and whistled in warning. Her stomach lurched as Amber soared over the hedge.

The mare never even broke stride. She landed smoothly on the other side and kept going. "Oh, Amber, you're incredible!" Linda cried.

They raced down a slope into a shallow, pebbly gulch, and then up the other side. A few seconds later, Linda caught sight of the paved road ahead. Reluctantly she reined Amber in.

Snorting and prancing, Amber came to a halt. She was breathing a little faster, but there was hardly a trace of sweat on her shiny neck. Linda slid off her back and hugged her.

"That was great," she said. "You must be the fastest horse in this county. Now let's see how long it takes Kathy and Patches to catch up with us."

Amber arched her neck and pricked her ears forward. "What are you doing, posing for the cameras?" Linda asked. "All right, it's true. You look like a statue—a beautiful golden statue."

Linda pulled Amber's reins over her head. Then, holding the knotted ends loosely in her hand, she sat down with her back against a tall ponderosa pine. "I wonder if there are any parts for horses in this film," she said. "I bet they'd cast you in a second, Amber.

"I wonder if there are any parts for me and Kathy," Linda went on wistfully. "Wouldn't that be great? What if there are some really big stars in this movie? I bet you we'll get to meet some famous people." She jumped to her feet, excited. "Maybe we'll even—"

"Hey, Linda! What's up—did you sit on a pinecone?" Kathy called as she jogged up on Patches.

Linda could feel herself blushing. "I guess I was just getting a little carried away," she admitted with a laugh. "I was thinking about us getting parts in this film and being discovered."

She put her foot into the stirrup and swung onto Amber's back. "But first we've got to find out what they're filming," she added. "Let's ride!"

"Maybe it's a romance," Kathy said hopefully. "I love romances."

"I know. You're such a softie," Linda teased. She

guided Amber around a boulder-strewn hollow in the ground. "*I* hope it's an adventure. You know, like one of those old-style westerns, with cowboys and rustlers and horses and rattlesnakes. That would be fun. And Amber would be sure to get a part in it." She grinned.

"I don't think they make those anymore," Kathy commented. "These days, all the bad guys ride around in black limousines. Like the bad guys on 'Diamond Street.'"

The girls rode up a pebbly rise. The tree line ended abruptly at the top. "Yeah. So what do you think did happen to Stephanie?" Linda asked. "I bet you a batch of chocolate chip cookies she was really kidnapped."

"You're on," Kathy said promptly. "And don't forget I like my cookies with walnuts in them. I'm almost positive she got away from those guys. I think she really ran away, and—" She broke off suddenly, staring at something.

"Linda! What's happening down there?" she cried, pointing.

They were at the top of the rise. Before them lay a wide, flat, treeless plain. Linda looked where Kathy was pointing. Her eyes widened.

There were three clouds of dust on the plain, about two hundred yards from the girls. The first one was being made by a compact chestnut quarter horse, who was galloping at top speed. Linda could just make out the rider through the dust—it looked like a girl around her age, with long dark hair streaming behind her.

The second cloud was being made by another horse, a big rangy buckskin. His rider was a tall, heavyset man. These two were following the girl.

The third cloud of dust was being made by a jeep, which was driving alongside the man on the buckskin. As Linda and Kathy stared, it pulled ahead until it was next to the girl on the quarter horse. Then it began swerving toward her.

The driver of the jeep was trying to cut her off!

"Hey!" Kathy cried, sounding scared.

"What—" Linda began. Then she saw the man on the buckskin uncoil a rope from the pommel of his saddle. He twirled it over his head.

"Come on!" Linda yelled, digging her heels into Amber's sides. "We've got to help that girl. I think those men are trying to kidnap her!"

2 ◆◆◆◆

"Hyaaah!" Linda shouted. Amber surged forward, her hoofs clattering on the pebbly slope. As they raced across the plain, Linda bent low over her horse's neck.

"Come on, Amber," she murmured. She squeezed Amber's flanks between her knees.

Amber must have caught Linda's urgency, for she responded with an unbelievable burst of speed. Linda rose in her stirrups like a jockey as they shot forward. In no time at all, they were drawing level with the man on the buckskin.

Out of the corner of her eye, Linda could see the man's startled expression as she and Amber pulled past him. She slapped her right rein against Amber's neck. Amber veered smoothly to the left—across the buckskin's path!

The buckskin's stride faltered for a moment. "Hey!" the man yelled. "What the—?"

Linda wheeled Amber and shot across the other horse's path again. With a panicky neigh, the buckskin swerved. But his rider kept going straight ahead.

Linda reined Amber in. She bit her lip as the man flew through the air. But, amazingly, the second he hit the ground he went into a shoulder roll. In a moment he was on his feet.

Glancing behind her, Linda caught sight of Kathy on Patches. It looked as though Kathy had tried to ride the pinto in front of the jeep, but Patches had balked. Now a man had jumped down from the jeep and was holding Patches's bridle. Kathy looked terrified.

"All right, kid!" the heavyset man growled. Linda's head snapped around at the sound of his voice. She swallowed hard as he strode toward her, but she stood her ground. She couldn't leave Kathy alone with these men.

"What's the big idea?" the man demanded. He glared at Linda. "Why did you ruin our take?"

Take? Linda wondered. "I wasn't about to sit there and let you kidnap that girl," she retorted. "You might as well give up right now. I'm sure she'll be back with the sheriff any second." Linda hoped she sounded surer than she felt.

Then the heavyset man burst out laughing! Linda stared at him, openmouthed, as he guffawed.

"Oh, man," he gasped. "That's the best thing I've heard in years! Hey, Lou, get over here! This kid thinks we're for real!"

The passenger door of the jeep flew open. A short, bald man with aviator glasses stepped out. "I don't care what she *thought,*" he snapped. "Young lady, do you realize what you've just done?"

Linda was taken aback. "I—"

"I suppose you thought it was all a joke," Lou went on. "Ha, ha, very funny. Well, you've just cost Hollywood thousands of dollars."

Hollywood! Linda cast a helpless look at Kathy, who had just ridden up to them. Kathy's eyes were round with astonishment. "But I didn't—" Linda began again.

"Oh, yes, you did!" Lou ranted. "Do you think these people"—he waved a hand at the man Linda had cut off—"work for free? This is Andy Hatfield. He's the best stuntman on television. We only hire the best for 'Diamond Street.' But they cost us. They cost us plenty!"

13

"'Diamond Street.'" Linda almost choked. "You mean—you mean you're filming 'Diamond Street' here in Lockwood?" she asked faintly.

"Wow," Kathy breathed.

Lou gave Linda a withering stare. "Don't tell me you haven't heard," he said sarcastically.

"Hey, Lou, maybe the kid didn't know," Andy said. "Give her a break. Look, here comes Joy back again." He pointed to the girl who had fled on horseback. She was riding toward them, looking amused. Linda could see now that she was really a woman in her midtwenties.

"We'll just shoot the scene over and make sure we get it right this time," Andy went on. "We'd have had to do another take anyway."

"I'm really sorry, sir," Linda put in. She could feel a blush burning her cheeks. "I just thought—"

"Spare me," Lou said, cutting her off.

Linda was vaguely aware of someone else getting out of the jeep and walking toward them. But mostly she was feeling like she wanted to sink into the ground. How could she have been such an idiot?

"Oh, my gosh." Kathy's awed voice broke into Linda's thoughts. "You're Joanna Curtiss. You play Stephanie!"

Linda looked more closely at the newcomer. Her

14

heart started to pound with excitement. Kathy was right! It was their favorite television star!

"I'm Kathy Hamilton," Kathy said breathlessly. "I just love your show!"

Joanna Curtiss was about thirteen or fourteen, with long black hair and blue eyes. Those eyes were cold now as she stared at Kathy. She flicked her glance over Linda, then turned to Lou.

"What's going on?" she demanded. "This is boring—I don't want to stay out in this jeep all day. Why can't we finish up? I want to go back to the hotel and rest."

"No problem, dear. We'll be done in no time. There was a little hitch, that's all." Lou pointed straight at Linda.

"This young lady here pulled a very foolish stunt and broke up our take." He gave Linda a tolerant smile. "Next time, dear, take a tip from your friend Kathy. Stay out of trouble."

Linda wanted to crawl under a rock and never come out. Never in her worst dreams had she been so completely embarrassed.

Lou clapped his hands. "Okay, people, from the top." He puffed out his chest and strode back to the jeep.

Joanna cast a single, contemptuous look at Linda.

"What a dumb move," she said. She turned and followed Lou.

"Oh, boy." Linda drew a long, shaky breath. She gathered the reins into her fist and turned Amber around. "Let's get out of here," she said to Kathy.

"Linda, did you see her? That was Joanna Curtiss!" Kathy called as she trotted after her friend.

"All I saw was that she thinks I'm an idiot. And she's right. Oh, Kathy, I feel so stupid!" Linda felt tears stinging her eyes.

"Well, how were you supposed to know it was only a shoot?" Kathy said loyally. "That man, Lou, didn't have to be so mean about it, either. You were only trying to help. It was an honest mistake. Although I'm glad Patches wouldn't move," she admitted.

Linda reached down and patted Amber's neck. "Well, you did great, girl, even if I made a stupid mistake," she said. She heaved a deep sigh. "A *really* stupid mistake."

"Oh, stop worrying," Kathy said. "No one will blame you. Wait until Amy and Marni hear that we met Joanna Curtiss. And 'Diamond Street,' right here in Lockwood. They're going to die!"

"Yeah," Linda said. She felt a little more cheerful. Kathy was right. It was exciting to have met a big TV star. And what had happened at the shoot really wasn't her fault. Was it?

They rode past Mr. Wyeth's gas station, at the edge of town. Then they turned right onto Villamar Road, where Amy and Marni Brown lived.

Linda and Kathy untacked their horses and put them in the corral with the Browns' horses. Linda noticed that their friend Kelly Michaels's horse, Cinder, was also there. Kelly was a couple of years older than the other girls, but she and Linda had become fast friends when Linda had helped her through some tough times with her family. Now Kelly was friends with Kathy and the Browns, too.

Amy, Marni, and Kelly were eating lunch in the kitchen of the Browns' big, Spanish-style house. Kelly jumped up when Linda and Kathy came in.

"Hey, have you heard about 'Diamond Street'?" she asked eagerly.

"Boy, have we," Kathy answered before Linda could open her mouth. "We ran into their shoot. We met Joanna Curtiss!"

"You're kidding!" Amy said, sounding impressed. "What happened?"

Kathy looked at Linda. "You tell them."

Linda explained what had happened. "I felt *so*

dumb," she concluded. "Joanna looked at me like I was some kind of insect. I'm glad they'll only be here for one show—I'd hate to run into her around Lockwood." She reached for a sandwich.

Kelly shook her blond head. "Sorry to tell you, but they're not leaving here for at least a week. My stepfather talked to one of the crew—he says they're going to shoot four episodes here."

"Oh, no!" Linda's heart sank.

"That's neat!" Marni exclaimed. "I mean, sorry, Linda, but it is kind of exciting. What else did your stepfather find out, Kelly?"

Kelly leaned forward. "Well, he found out what happens on the show. Stephanie ran away to here, you know."

Kathy poked Linda. "You owe me cookies."

"She's staying with a nice old lady who's helping her to hide from those guys in the black limo. I bet the scene you messed up was the one where they spot her and try to kidnap her again."

"This is great!" Kathy said through a mouthful of peanut butter and jelly. "Now we don't have to wait till September to find out what happened. Hey, do you think they'll really be looking for extras?"

Kelly shrugged. "Let's go over to the Huntington Hotel and ask."

"All right!" Amy said. She got up and carried her plate to the sink.

Linda looked at her half-eaten sandwich. Her stomach felt full of butterflies. She wasn't at all sure she wanted to face Joanna Curtiss or Lou right now.

They all went out to the corral and saddled up. Linda swung onto Amber's back and fidgeted with the reins for a second. What should she do?

"I don't think I'll go, you guys," she said finally. "I promised Doña I'd weed the garden for her this afternoon." This wasn't exactly true. She'd promised to do it by the next afternoon, but she didn't want her friends to think she was just being a party pooper.

"Oh, Linda, can't you do it later?" Kathy asked. "This is going to be so much fun. What if we all get parts?"

It did sound great. Linda hesitated for a second. But then she thought of Joanna Curtiss's scornful expression.

She shook her head. "I really should go home," she said regretfully. "Maybe they'll have parts to hand out tomorrow, too."

"Maybe." Kathy gave Linda a doubtful look. "Well, I guess we'll see you later, then."

"Yeah, see you later," Amy chimed in.

"Have a good time, you guys," Linda said. She wheeled Amber and rode away.

"I guess I'm making a big deal out of nothing, huh, Amber?" she mused as they jogged along Villamar Road. "After all, what I did made sense, in a way. How was I supposed to know they were filming a scene? I didn't see any cameras or anything. Did you?"

Amber nickered.

Linda chuckled. "You're tired of hearing about it, aren't you, girl. Well, I'm tired of thinking about it, too. So let's forget it." She snapped her fingers. "I know! We'll work on that new jump, that capriole."

Recently, Doña and Bronco—Linda's grandfather—had taken Linda and Bob into Los Angeles. A troop of Lippizaner stallions had been performing there, and they'd all gone to see them.

Linda had fallen in love with the stately white horses. Of course, they weren't as wonderful as Amber, but they did do amazing tricks. She'd wanted to try some with Amber ever since. She'd even checked some books on Lippizaners out of the Lockwood library.

Thinking about the Lippizaners now, Linda began to feel a lot more cheerful. "So what if they're casting extras for 'Diamond Street'?" she said aloud. "I have other things to do. Right, Amber?" Smiling, she squeezed the mare's flanks with her knees. Amber swung into a smooth lope.

Eager to try the new trick, Linda pointed her horse back to Rancho del Sol. As they approached the ranch, Linda slowed Amber to a walk, then halted her by a stand of ponderosa pines. She gazed at the sight before her.

The ranch house was a long, low, rambling building made of whitewashed stucco, with a red tile roof. It looked like a Spanish mission.

It stood on a very slight rise. In front of it, a lush green lawn sloped down to the barn, corral, and outbuildings. Off in the west, Linda could see rolling foothills. A single eagle soared high above her head.

Linda drew in a long breath. Rancho del Sol was indeed beautiful. She couldn't think of any place she'd rather grow up.

Amber stamped her feet and flicked at a fly with her tail. "Restless?" Linda asked her. "Okay, let's go."

She rode into the barn. At this time of day, Mac and all the hands were out on the range. The outbuildings were quiet and empty.

Linda dismounted and led Amber to the hitching post. She quickly unsaddled the mare and pulled off her bridle. She took a body brush and gave Amber's coat a once-over. Amber snorted with pleasure as the brush tickled her back. Then Linda buckled on Amber's rope halter and snapped a lunge line to it.

"Just wait here one second, okay, Amber?" Linda said as she led the mare outside. She looped the lunge rope over one of the corral posts. "I want to go up to the house and get some goodies for you."

Linda ran across the lawn to the kitchen door. "Doña?" she called. She pushed open the bottom half of the Dutch door. "I'm back."

"Oh, Linda, there you are." Luisa Alvarez, the Mallorys' housekeeper, bustled into the kitchen, tying on an apron. "Doña's still out. I'm starting dinner now—with all those new hands, I swear it takes me all day just to put food in their stomachs."

"Poor Luisa," Linda said with a grin. "You know you love doing it."

Luisa drew herself up to her full five feet. "I'll have no back talk from you, young lady," she said with mock severity. "Out of my kitchen! Oh, Kathy called. She wanted you to call her back right away."

"Really? I just left her a couple of hours ago." Linda hurried into the den and picked up the phone there. She dialed Kathy's number quickly.

"Linda!" Kathy cried as soon as Linda said hello.

"You'll never guess what happened with 'Diamond Street'!"

"Did you get a part? Are you an extra?" Linda asked eagerly. "Tell me everything!"

"Am I an *extra*? No." Kathy paused dramatically. "I got a *speaking* part!"

3 ♦♦♦♦

As she heard Kathy's news, Linda felt a stab of envy. What had she missed by not going with her friends that afternoon? Maybe *she* could have had that part!

Then she realized how selfish she was being. "Kathy, that's fantastic," she said. "I can't believe how lucky you are! How did it happen? What kind of part is it?"

"Well," Kathy admitted, "I have only three lines, but they're good ones. I'm the friendly town girl who hides Stephanie in the closet when the bad guys are searching for her. I get to say, 'Climb in here,' 'I've never even heard of her,' and 'If you're not out of here in five seconds, I'm going to call the police.'"

"Wow." Linda tried not to sound envious. Those three lines sounded pretty great to her. "So, how did it happen?" she prompted.

24

"See, they had a professional actress all set to play this part," Kathy explained. "But she backed out at the last minute—I think she got a part in a cereal commercial. So they were stuck. And they asked me to read the lines for them, and I did, and they gave me this form for my parents to sign, and then they gave me the part." She gave a happy sigh. "I still can't believe it."

Linda grinned. "You're totally lucky, Kath."

"Oh, and you know what else? After I got the part, Joanna Curtiss came up and congratulated me. She wasn't stuck-up at all. I think she's great."

"Wow," Linda said again, wistfully.

"She even said she'd go over the scene with me sometime."

"Neat! Hey, what about Amy and Marni and Kelly? Did they get anything?"

"Yeah, they're all in a couple of crowd scenes. . . . Okay, Mom, I'll be right there!" Kathy shouted. Linda held the phone away from her ear.

"I've got to go—Mom needs help in the restaurant," Kathy said. The Hamiltons ran a busy restaurant right outside of Lockwood.

"Okay, I'll see you later," Linda said.

"You know, you should go over to the Huntington

tomorrow morning. I think they're still looking for extras."

"Okay, I will," Linda promised. "Maybe I'll get lucky, too. We could be in a scene together."

"Maybe," Kathy said with a laugh. "But I think it's just Stephanie, the bad guys, and me in our scene. Sorry."

"Oh, well. I'll call you tomorrow." Linda hung up. She was a little hurt. Kathy didn't sound as if she cared whether or not they had a scene together.

Linda grabbed a handful of carrots and walked slowly down to the corral. Amber was still waiting patiently at the gate.

"Sorry I left you here so long," Linda said. She pressed her cheek against Amber's neck. "Oh, Amber, I should have gone with those guys. Do you think I blew my chances?"

Amber turned her head and nibbled gently at Linda's sleeve. Then she delicately picked up the lunge rope with her teeth. She shook it.

"You're right," Linda said, straightening up. "We have work to do. Besides, there's always tomorrow. Okay, let's try our new trick."

She led Amber to the middle of the corral. Holding the twenty-foot rope in one hand, she clucked her tongue. That was Amber's signal. The mare began to trot, making a wide circle with Linda at the center. Linda turned slowly to follow the mare. Amber's strides were long and fluid.

"Now canter!" Linda called. Amber shifted into a clean, rocking lope.

"Looks real good," a man's voice called. Linda looked over her shoulder and saw Mac, the foreman, leaning over the corral gate. His big bay horse, Stormy, was ground-tied beside him.

Linda smiled, feeling a glow of pride. Mac didn't give praise a lot, but when he did, you knew he really meant it.

"Whoa, Amber," she called. Dropping the lunge line, she ran over to the gate. "Hi!"

"Hey, slow down." Mac's blue eyes crinkled as he smiled. "What's your rush?"

"I've been trying to teach Amber a capriole," Linda told him. "I've taught her to relax on the lunge, but so far I can't get her to leap on command. Do you have a minute?"

"A minute," Mac said, looking at his watch, "but not much more. I've got to check the south fences today."

"Can you watch us and tell us what we're doing wrong?"

"A capriole, huh?" Mac shoved his cowboy hat

back on his head. "That's one of those flying leaps, right? Pretty fancy stuff. Don't know as I can tell you too much about those Lippizaner tricks. But I'll try."

"Thanks, Mac." Linda raced into the barn and got her grandfather's carriage whip out of the tack room. Not that she would ever dream of hitting Amber with it. She only used it as a signal, snapping it when she wanted Amber to leap.

She returned to the corral. "Okay, here goes," she said to Amber. "Ready?"

She clucked and Amber began to trot. At Linda's command, she broke into a canter. Linda took a deep breath. This was the hard part, coming up.

She raised the whip and cracked the long lash in the air. Amber faltered for a second, then picked up her stride again.

Shaking her head, Linda called to Amber to halt. Then she turned to Mac. "See what I mean?" she said. "I don't know how to make Amber understand what she's supposed to do when I crack the whip."

Mac frowned. "I see your problem. But I don't know what the answer is." He checked his watch again. "Tell you what," he said. "I have to go now, but I'll sleep on it. You think it over, too, and tomorrow we'll put our heads together and see what we can do."

"Okay, thanks, Mac."

Mac picked up the reins and swung easily into Stormy's saddle. "So long," he called, and rode away.

Linda turned to Amber. "Well, girl, it's just you and me," she said. Amber nickered. "We can do it, Amber. I know we can!" Linda shook the lunge rope. "We just have to keep trying."

She put Amber through the trot, then the canter again. "Now, here it comes," she called to the palomino. "Are you ready? Up!"

At the same time, Linda cracked the whip. Amber put her head down, hunched her back, and hopped into the air.

"That's it!" Linda cheered. It wasn't a real leap, but a crowhop was better than nothing. "One more time, girl. Up!"

Once again, Amber hopped. This time she kicked up her heels a little and snorted.

"All *right!*" Linda cried. She halted Amber and gave her a carrot. Amber lipped it delicately from Linda's flat palm, then crunched it up.

They kept at it for the rest of the afternoon. Amber didn't hop every single time, but when she did, Linda made sure to reward her with a chunk of carrot. A hop wasn't a leap, but it was certainly a good start.

"Okay, girl, I guess we've had enough," Linda

finally said. She took Amber into the barn and gave her a long, thorough grooming. Then she poured a heaping measure of oats into the trough. She didn't often overfeed Amber, but today was special.

By the time Linda finished, it was just six o'clock. Bob, her older brother, came into the barn as she was putting away her brushes.

"Hey," he greeted her. He ducked his head to walk through the tack room door.

Bob was fifteen and lanky, with blond hair and blue eyes. He wasn't really all *that* tall, but he had grown a lot over the past year. Now he liked to pretend he was too tall to fit through the doorways. Linda thought that was pretty dumb.

"Hey, yourself," she said. "Are Doña and Bronco back yet?"

Bob nodded. "They just got here. Where were you all day, anyway? I was the only one here for lunch."

"Nowhere special," Linda mumbled. She didn't really feel like talking about the "Diamond Street" disaster.

Bob took the grain measure down. "I'm going into town tomorrow. I heard they're looking for extras on that TV show they're filming here."

"Uh-huh. Well, see you up at the house," Linda said quickly. She hurried out of the barn, stopping only to look in on Amber. The palomino snorted contentedly from her stall.

Linda went up to the ranch house. As she passed the living room, she stuck in her head. Doña was there. So was Bronco, Linda's grandfather.

"Well, hello, there!" Bronco called out when he saw Linda. "How's our movie star?"

Linda could feel herself blushing. "I'm not a movie star. I didn't even go to the casting."

Bronco and Doña exchanged surprised glances. "Why not, dear?" asked Doña.

"Um, it's a long story," Linda began. Then the dinner bell rang.

"Go and wash your hands, and you can tell us over dinner," Doña said.

"Okay." Linda ran upstairs and washed her hands and face. Then she walked slowly downstairs and slid into her place at the dining room table. She wasn't really looking forward to telling her family about her morning.

Bob tromped in and sat down. "The air smells kind of smoky outside. Is there a forest fire nearby or something?" He reached for a platter of chicken.

Bronco ran a hand through his silver hair. "There *is* one not too far west of us," he said, sounding worried. "Glen Manlon was telling me about it this

31

afternoon. It seems the rangers were doing a controlled burn in the state park to get rid of some deadwood, and some wind spread it faster than they'd intended."

"A fire?" Linda said, her eyes wide. "But it's only June. Fires don't usually start up until July or August, do they?"

"That's the natural season, honey," Bronco answered. "But we got less than normal rainfall last winter and spring. I guess the land is just dried out."

Now Doña looked concerned, too. Laying down her fork, she asked, "How far west? It's not coming this way, is it, Tom?" Tom was Bronco's real name, but no one ever called him that—except Doña.

"Not so far. It hasn't hit the mountains yet. Unless the wind shifts, we should be fine here. Don't you worry," Bronco told her.

"Wow, a forest fire! If it comes this way, I want to volunteer for the fire fighters," Bob declared.

"They won't take you," Linda informed him. "You're not old enough. Or tall enough." She grinned at him and took a bite of chicken.

"Yeah, yeah," Bob muttered. "We'll see."

"We *won't* see," Doña said firmly. "The fire's on the other side of the mountains, and that's where it'll stay, if I have anything to say about it. Now, Linda, tell us about this famous movie shoot.''

"Oh, that." Linda looked down at her plate. "Well, here's what happened. . . ."

Linda told them everything. When she got to the part about knocking Andy Hatfield off his horse, Bob burst out laughing.

"You did that?" he exclaimed. "Boy, he must have been surprised. That's great riding—for a girl, anyway."

Now that Linda thought about it, she could see that Bob was right. It *was* great riding. She gave him a look. "I guess you think you and Rocket could have done better?" she retorted.

Doña and Bronco were laughing, too. "I'm sorry, honey," Bronco said, wiping his eyes, "but I wish I'd been there to see that man's face."

Linda smiled. It *was* pretty funny, come to think of it. Even Andy Hatfield had laughed, and he was the one who had been knocked off his horse!

Maybe it wasn't a total disaster. Maybe Joanna Curtiss didn't really think she was an idiot. Maybe she'd worried much too much about the whole thing.

"Anyway," she finished up, "I didn't go to the Huntington with Kathy and everybody. I was too embarrassed. But I think I'll go in tomorrow. Kathy says they're still looking for extras. She even got some lines to say."

"That's incredible," Bob said. "Hey, you can ride in with me if you want. I'm meeting Larry at his house."

"Okay," Linda agreed. Excitement was bubbling up inside her again. Tomorrow was going to be a great day. She could feel it!

"Look!" Linda whispered to Bob and Larry. "There's Joanna Curtiss."

It was the next morning. Bob and Linda had gotten up early to pick up Bob's best friend, Larry Spencer, at his house. Now the three of them were sitting on their horses outside the Huntington Hotel, waiting for the casting director to come out. They weren't the only ones—a small crowd waited with them.

Joanna Curtiss came out first. She was with a thin, tanned, blond woman in her thirties. Joanna's eye caught Linda's. Linda gave a tentative wave, hoping Joanna would recognize her.

Joanna's blue eyes narrowed for a second, but then she smiled. She touched the blond woman's arm and said something to her. Both of them looked straight at Linda.

"She saw me," Linda said excitedly. "She remembers who I am."

"How could she forget?" Larry teased. He poked Linda in the ribs. "You cost Hollywood thousands of dollars."

"Quit that, Larry!" Linda protested. "I think that lady is the casting director. Maybe she's going to pick us."

The blond woman held up her hands for silence. "I'm Susan Carson," she announced when it was quiet. "I'm casting a few extra roles today, as you all seem to know already."

The crowd cheered.

Ms. Carson beckoned to Bob. "You," she called. "Over here, please."

With a wide grin for Linda and Larry, Bob dismounted and walked over to the porch. Linda held her breath. Who would be next?

Ms. Carson pointed at Larry. "You, too."

"All right!" Larry crowed. He slid off the back of his Appaloosa, Snowbird. "Good luck," he said to Linda.

Now Ms. Carson was pointing at Linda. Her heart pounding with excitement, Linda dismounted. "I'll ask about horse roles," she promised Amber. Amber tossed her head.

"That's a lovely palomino you have there," Ms. Carson said as Linda walked up the porch steps.

Linda beamed with pride. "Thank you. She's very smart, too. I've even taught her some tricks."

"As a matter of fact, that's why I wanted to see you," the casting director said.

"It is?"

"Yes. I think we have a part for her."

Linda's heart skipped a beat. "Wh-what about me?" she ventured.

"Well, Joanna points out that you resemble her a bit too much in height and coloring. It might confuse the viewers if we shot the two of you together. But I do need a smart, good-looking, well-trained horse. Joanna says your palomino is just right." Ms. Carson beamed. Joanna gave Linda a strange smile.

So *that* was what they had been talking about. Linda's heart sank.

"What do you need Amber for?" she heard herself asking.

Ms. Carson looked surprised. "Why, for Joanna to ride, of course!"

4 ◆◆◆◆

"But I thought you already had a horse for the riding scenes," Linda blurted. Then, not wanting to hurt Amber's chances, she added quickly, "But I'm sure Amber could do it, if you really need her."

Ms. Carson frowned. "We're going to reshoot the riding footage. There were . . . problems with several of the shots. The horse we first chose wasn't all that well trained." She shot Joanna a sharp glance.

Linda wondered about that look. Did Ms. Carson think Joanna Curtiss had something to do with the problem shots? Maybe Joanna wasn't such a good rider.

"Well, Amber's the best," Linda said loyally. "But she isn't used to anyone but me riding her. Maybe I'd better be around for the shooting, in case there are any problems."

"I don't need a baby-sitter!" Joanna said nastily. Then she gave a syrupy smile. "I mean," she added in a sweet voice, "if *you* can ride Amber, I'm sure I can, too. I've had years of training, you know."

"We're sure you ride very well, Joanna," Ms. Carson cut in soothingly. "Then I take it the matter is settled?"

Linda nodded, trying not to let her disappointment show. She was feeling left out. Everyone had a part in "Diamond Street" except for her!

"Good. I'll need to make arrangements with Amber's legal owners," Ms. Carson said briskly. "Would that be your parents, Linda?"

"No, my grandparents. Bronc—Tom and Rosalinda Mallory." Linda gave Ms. Carson her home telephone number.

"Thank you. We won't need Amber until tomorrow morning, so that gives us plenty of time to do the paperwork. Can you have Amber here at eight-thirty in the morning?"

Linda nodded.

"Fine." Ms. Carson turned to Bob and Larry. "Yes, you two should be just right for the crowd of boys. You can pick up schedules and release forms from that gentleman over there." She gestured to a young man sitting at a table piled high with papers.

A Star in the Saddle

"Great. Thanks," Bob said. He nudged Larry.

"Yeah, thanks." Larry looked at Joanna. "Um, my kid sister would really love to have your autograph," he said.

Linda nearly burst out laughing. That Larry! He didn't have a sister. He wanted Joanna's autograph for himself.

"Let's go, Larry," Bob said, leading his friend away.

Linda followed them. "Wait up!" she called.

"Hey, Linda, I'm sorry you can't be in the show, too," Bob said. His blue eyes were sympathetic as he reached out and tousled his sister's hair.

Linda shrugged. "Yeah, well . . ." she said. But she felt a little better.

"Just sign these," the young man at the table told Larry and Bob. He held out sheets of paper and pens to them. "And here's one for you, too, miss." He started to hand one to Linda.

"No, I don't need one," she told him. "I'm not allowed in any of the scenes. I look too much like Joanna Curtiss."

The young man raised his eyebrows. "That must be a new rule. I've never heard it before. I'll tell you, the trouble that girl causes around here. . . ." he muttered.

"Hey, Linda!"

Linda turned. Kathy was threading her way through the crowd. She came up to Linda.

"Can you believe this mob?" she asked. "All these people, hoping to get little tiny extra roles. Joanna says most of the crowd footage gets cut in the final edit, anyway."

"Gee, that's too bad. I hope none of our friends gets cut," Linda said.

"Yeah. But you never know. Say, did they give you a part? Joanna said they probably wouldn't, since you kind of look like her."

"She was right," Linda said briefly. She was thinking about the guy at the form table. He had said Joanna made up that rule. It certainly seemed as if Joanna didn't like Linda Craig.

"Hi, Kathy. I hear you're going to be a star," Bob said. He and Larry walked up, holding their schedules.

"Well, sort of." Kathy blushed. Sometimes Linda suspected Kathy had a crush on Bob, although Kathy always denied it.

"Do you really have a whole scene with Joanna Curtiss?" Larry put in. Kathy nodded proudly.

"Well, well, aren't we special," Bob teased. "Put in a good word for us, okay?"

"Okay. But my scene isn't until the day after tomorrow. Of course, I'll probably be talking to Joanna between now and then," Kathy said grandly.

"Listen," Linda said. "None of us has anything to do today. Does anybody feel like going on a picnic? We could ride out to Coyote Mountain."

"Um, well—wait! Let me see that schedule a second, Larry." Kathy pulled the scene list from Larry's hands and scanned it.

"Joanna doesn't have any scenes this afternoon," Kathy announced after a few seconds. "I'm going to invite her along."

Linda was dismayed. "Do you think she'd want to come?" she asked Kathy doubtfully.

Kathy frowned at Linda. "I don't see why not," she said. "Joanna's not a snob or anything."

"I didn't mean that."

"I'll ask her right now." Kathy hurried to the hotel porch.

To Linda's surprise, Joanna seemed eager to come along. "But I don't have a horse," she explained. "Someone will have to lend me one."

"No problem," Bob declared. "You can use one of ours. Come on, you can ride double with me to our ranch."

41

Linda's eyes widened. She didn't think Joanna would want to share a ride with anyone.

But Joanna smiled her thanks. "That's really nice of you."

Maybe I misjudged her, Linda thought. She unlooped Amber's reins from the porch railing and mounted. Joanna was acting really nice.

Kathy rode behind Linda until they got to the Hamiltons' house. There she saddled up Patches.

As the group continued to Rancho del Sol, Linda felt left out of the conversation. No one was talking to her. Every time she opened her mouth, it seemed as if Joanna had something more important to say.

All she talked about was her life in Hollywood. How she had her own chauffeur-driven limousine. How she didn't have to go to school but had a private tutor. How she lived in a gigantic mansion with tons of servants. After a while, Linda began to suspect Joanna was making some of it up.

Then, as they neared Ranch del Sol, Joanna started gushing about *that*. "What a neat place!" she kept saying. "Oh, Bob, you're so *lucky* to live here!"

"What about me?" Linda muttered. "I live here, too." But only Amber heard her.

They rode to the south pasture. "Here, take your pick," Bob told Joanna. He waved his hand at a knot of horses grazing in the long grass. "Any horse you want."

Joanna slid off Rocket's back and walked to the fence. "How about that one?" She pointed at a spirited gray stallion who was frisking by himself.

"El Capitán? Okay. I'll get him." Bob gathered up his reins. "Linda, could you open the gate for me?"

"Uh, Bob, I think we ought to get permission first," Linda said. She hated to sound like a spoilsport, but El Capitán was a Paso Fino stallion—a very valuable horse. Linda knew Bronco and Doña were very strict about who rode him.

"Oh, Bob, *please?*" Joanna begged. She giggled. "I promise I'll treat him like a king."

Linda winced. *Yuck!* she thought. I hope Bob doesn't fall for that! "That's not the point," she said aloud. "He's very spirited."

Bob glared at Linda. "I'm sure Joanna can handle Cap," he said. "Anyway, Bronco and Doña aren't home right now."

Bob was right—both cars were gone from the driveway. Linda didn't want to start an argument. She leaned down and unlatched the gate.

"Yee-haw!" Bob shouted. "Come on, Larry!"

Both boys tore through the gate. Larry wheeled his Appaloosa, Snowbird, and made him rear. Snowbird's ears lay flat against his head—he hated being yanked around that way. Then Bob waved his hat in the air, and they galloped over to the bewildered-looking herd.

Linda shook her head. Larry was too reckless. He was lucky he'd never been seriously hurt.

"Oh, look, Kathy," Joanna said, squealing. "Aren't they the greatest riders?"

Linda could hardly believe her ears when Kathy breathlessly agreed. "The best. Right, Linda?"

"I—" Linda began. Joanna cut her off.

"Larry is so in control. And Bob—he's kind of cute, don't you think?"

Joanna was totally ignoring Linda! What was worse, Kathy didn't even seem to notice. Linda had had enough.

"I'm going to get some food," she said, trying to keep the anger out of her voice. "Anyone want to help?"

Kathy turned to go with Linda. But Joanna reached up and caught Patches's bridle.

"Stay here with me, Kathy," she pleaded. "Linda doesn't mind getting the food by herself. Do you, Linda?" She smiled sweetly.

Linda was too angry to reply. She just wheeled,

shook the reins, and sent Amber flying up the lawn to the house.

"Ay!" cried Luisa, when she saw them appear at the Dutch door to the kitchen. "I thought you were about to crash through the house on that beast, from all the noise. What's wrong?"

"Everything," Linda grumbled. She jumped down and opened the door. "Sorry if I scared you. Is it okay if I take some of the leftovers from last night? We're going on a picnic."

"Sure. You want some lemon juice to drink? I think that would fit your mood."

That made Linda laugh. "Maybe I should take some along for everyone else, to stop them from being so sappy," she joked.

Linda grabbed some fried chicken, a bag of tortilla chips, some cans of soda, and five oranges. "There, that should be enough," she said.

"Here." Luisa held out an apple. "For that horse of yours."

Luisa was terrified of horses. She liked Amber— but strictly from a distance. Still, she was always giving Linda treats for the golden mare.

"Thanks, Luisa," Linda said. She grinned. "Sure you don't want to give it to her yourself?"

Luisa made a face. "Run along."

"See you later!" Linda stuffed the food into her saddlebags and rode to the barn. Bob had just finished tightening El Capitán's girth. He gave Joanna a leg up, and they were off.

As they rode, Linda's spirits began to lighten. It was a beautiful day. The wind blew gently in her face and rustled the leaves of the trees. Amber startled a flock of blackbirds, which rose into the air with a clatter of flapping wings. A white-tailed deer bounded across the path. It was the kind of day where troubles seemed to vanish, Linda thought.

Linda could see that Joanna was having trouble with El Capitán—he kept skittering off the trail. Then Joanna would yank on the reins to pull him back. She wasn't a very good Western rider.

Determined to be friendly, Linda moved up alongside her. "You usually ride English, don't you?" she asked.

Joanna's back stiffened. "Of course I do. It's the civilized way to ride," she snapped. "But I can ride Western perfectly well."

Linda sighed. So much for friendliness.

After a while they passed an orange trail marker. "That's where Rancho del Sol ends, isn't it, Bob?" Kathy asked.

Linda felt a pang. *Why didn't Kathy ask* me *that?* she wondered.

"Yes. And I smell smoke!" Bob called back. He and Larry were in the lead, scouting out the trail. "The forest fire must have hit the western slopes. We'd better stop—we don't want to get too close."

"Oh, come on, Bob, don't be such a chicken!" Joanna cried. "Let's go closer. Maybe we'll get to see the fire. I bet that's what Larry wants to do. Right, Larry?"

"Huh?" Larry looked around, confused. "Gee, Joanna, I don't know. We really shouldn't . . ."

"What? You're *both* scared? Fine—we can go without you," Joanna taunted them.

"Um, I . . . well, I guess we could go up to the rimrock," Kathy quavered. She looked scared.

"What?" Linda was aghast. "Kathy, don't be dumb. If we were on the rimrock and heavy smoke rolled in, we could be in big trouble. We'd be lost. And besides, if our families found out where we'd been, they'd kill us!"

"Spoilsport. No one said *you* had to come," Joanna muttered. But Bob was nodding.

"Linda's right," he said firmly. "A forest fire isn't something to play with. Come on, there's a nice clearing by that creek over there. Let's stop."

"Oh, all right. If *you* say so," Joanna grumbled. Kathy and Larry looked relieved.

Over lunch, Joanna's high spirits returned. Kathy, Bob, and Larry sat entranced as she told them more Hollywood stories. Linda just tried not to get annoyed.

". . . and everyone in Hollywood goes to Maxie's," Joanna was saying. "I've been there millions of times myself. Lots of times I just stop in during a break in a shoot. They all know me there."

"I thought kids couldn't go without their parents," Kathy said, with an admiring sigh.

Joanna made a scornful face. "It all depends on who you are," she said.

"Give me a break," Linda muttered. She had a feeling Joanna wasn't as much of a regular at Maxie's restaurant as she wanted them to think.

Bob frowned at Linda, and she felt herself flushing. But she returned his look defiantly. Can't you see Joanna's a phony? she wanted to shout.

"Sounds like your life is really something," Bob said to Joanna. He leaned back on his elbows and stuck a piece of grass in his mouth. "Say, do you have your own horse?"

"Horse? Try *horses*," Joanna boasted. "I've got three. And they're all Thoroughbreds."

"Wow!" Larry whistled. "Do you race them, or show them, or anything?"

Joanna smirked. "I've won several ribbons."

"What in?" Linda wanted to know.

Joanna suddenly looked uncomfortable. "Oh . . . this and that," she answered vaguely. "You know, different things."

She jumped up. "Come on, let's get going. I have to get back to the Huntington—they worry about me if I'm gone too long."

Larry helped Linda gather up the remains of their lunch, and then they untied the horses. Linda pulled a wad of grass out from behind Amber's bit. "You know you should never eat with a bit in your mouth," she scolded. "It's messy."

Amber hung her head. "Well, I guess you got hungry, too, huh, girl?" Linda laughed. Then she lengthened the stirrups and mounted.

Linda looked over to see if the others were ready to go, too. Joanna was standing in front of El Capitán, nodding at something Bob was asking.

"Sure I know Annie Ziga," she said. Annie Ziga was the lead singer of one of Bob's favorite rock bands. "We're good friends. I see her all the time."

"You're kidding!" Bob looked truly starstruck.

"I'm serious!" Joanna grinned. "Want to see my

49

imitation of Annie singing 'Panic in L.A.'?"

El Capitán shied as Joanna flailed her arms. " 'We-e-ell, there's trouble in the streets,' " she sang. Then she let out an earsplitting shriek. " *'Trouble!'* " she cried.

El Capitán neighed wildly. For a second he danced backward. Then he rose up on his hind legs, pawing the air.

And Joanna was right under his lashing hooves!

5 ◆◆◆◆

"Look out!" Linda yelled. Joanna just stood there. She looked paralyzed with fear.

"Go, Amber!" Linda kicked Amber forward and swept past El Capitán. She held the reins in her right hand, and with her left she reached down and grabbed Joanna's arm. Joanna stumbled after Amber as the golden mare threw herself clear of El Capitán's hooves.

And not a moment too soon! The gray came crashing down on the spot where Joanna had been standing. He gave a stiff-legged little hop. Then he stood still, though his entire body was trembling.

Amber snorted and pranced nervously. "Good girl, you did great," Linda whispered.

Bob moved cautiously forward. "Easy, Cap," he crooned. "Easy, boy. It's all right."

He reached out and took El Capitán's reins. "Wow, you really threw a fit," he murmured.

"Joanna, are you okay?" Kathy asked.

"F-fine." Joanna pulled her arm away from Linda's grasp and straightened up. "Thanks," she said shortly.

She brushed some dust off the leg of her designer jeans. "I guess Cap was spooked, huh?"

"You could say that," Linda put in. "You've got to be careful around stallions, especially if you don't know them. They can be very high-strung," she added, trying to be tactful.

Joanna shrugged her shoulders. "Thanks for the advice," she said in a slightly sarcastic voice. "But it came out all right, didn't it? I'm okay—it's no big deal. Right?"

That made Linda angry. It *was* a big deal! "Maybe not to you," she retorted. "But El Capitán could have hurt himself, too, you know. He's my grandmother's favorite, and he's important to the ranch. Did you ever think about that?"

There was a silence. Joanna's eyes blazed with fury for a second. Then suddenly her lower lip trembled.

"You're right," Joanna said. She looked utterly downcast. "It was all my fault. And I was only thinking about myself—as usual." She kicked at a clump of buffalo grass with her expensive-looking snakeskin boot.

"That wasn't what I meant," Linda began. She felt confused.

"No, you are right. Isn't she, Bob?" Joanna turned to Linda's brother, looking at him with big, sad eyes.

Bob rolled his eyes. "Linda," he said, "keep quiet—you're only making things worse. Let's go."

Linda opened her mouth, then shut it again. She hadn't meant to hurt Joanna's feelings like that. Everything had gotten turned around suddenly. It was so confusing!

Silently, everybody mounted up. El Capitán flinched a little as Joanna climbed into the saddle, but Bob held the reins until the stallion seemed calm again.

"Okay, troops, fall in," Larry ordered. Linda could tell he was trying to make everyone feel better. She smiled at him. Good old Larry.

They set out for Rancho del Sol. Larry led the way, with Kathy and Joanna single file behind him. Bob followed, and Linda brought up the rear.

As they rode, Bob gradually dropped back until he and Linda were riding side by side.

He looked angrily at her. "You were awfully hard on Joanna," he said in an accusing tone. "She didn't spook Cap on purpose."

"I know that," Linda protested. "I never said she meant to do it."

"Well, it sure sounded like that to the rest of us," Bob replied. "What's your problem, anyway? You've been a real sourpuss all day."

"I have?" Linda bit her lip. "I'm sorry. It's just that—"

She broke off, frustrated. How could she explain?

"Hey, Bob!" Larry's voice came from ahead of them. He reined Snowbird in. "Come check out this monster lizard. Want us to catch it for you, Joanna?"

"Ugh, a lizard!" Joanna squealed. "Boys are so disgusting, aren't they, Kathy?"

Bob dug his heels into Rocket's sides and clattered forward. Linda sighed.

"He wouldn't have listened to me anyway," she murmured. She leaned down and stroked Amber's silky neck. "Amber, why do I feel as if I did everything wrong?"

Amber tossed her head, making the bridle jingle.

"Larry, get that disgusting thing away from us," Kathy cried. Linda looked up. Larry had scooped up a big lizard that had been sunning itself on a rock. He was holding it out to Joanna.

"Eeeeeeekkk!" Joanna shrieked. El Capitán danced nervously sideways.

If she's not careful, Cap will spook again, Linda thought with alarm. She reined Amber in.

Now Joanna was giggling. "You guys are incredible," she said. "How could you even touch that thing, Larry?"

"Touch a lizard?" Bob broke in. "That's nothing. Watch this."

He grabbed the terrified reptile from Larry and held it up to his face. The lizard's forked tongue darted out and flicked his cheek.

"See?" he boasted. "They're harmless." He handed the lizard back to Larry, who set it down. It scuttled behind a rock.

Joanna and Kathy looked at each other. "Double yuck!" they shrieked in unison. Then they both exploded in giggles.

Linda sat on Amber's back and watched. She felt left out again. Especially when she caught Kathy's eye, and Kathy just looked away after a second, as if she hadn't seen Linda at all.

Joanna saw the exchange, though. As they started

moving again, she turned in her saddle and threw Linda a smug, triumphant smile.

Linda gasped as the truth hit her. Joanna must have gone through the whole I-was-wrong act just to get Kathy and the boys on her side. I can't believe it! Linda thought.

Furious, she squeezed Amber's flanks with her knees. Amber whinnied, then leapt forward. Her stride lengthened and she passed the others where the trail widened.

Linda could hear Bob shout her name as they shot by Rocket, but she didn't turn around. She just flew across the field toward home.

Later that afternoon, Linda went out to the corral to work on the capriole with Amber.

Kathy, Larry, and Joanna were all gone now. When they left, Linda hadn't even said goodbye. She had still been too mad about Joanna's trick to care whether or not anyone was mad at *her*. But now she was beginning to feel bad about being in a fight with Kathy. After all, Kathy didn't know that Joanna was such a faker.

"What should I do, Amber?" she asked aloud.

Amber gazed steadily at Linda, her dark eyes soft and gentle.

"I guess I should call Kathy and talk about it, huh?" Linda said with a sigh. Amber pricked her ears forward.

"You think that's the smartest thing I've said all day," Linda teased. "Okay, I'll do it!" She snapped the lunge rope onto Amber's halter, feeling a little better.

Someone cleared his throat behind her. "Talking to yourself?" came a deep voice.

Linda turned. "Mac! Hi." She blushed.

"Howdy." The foreman grinned at her. "I guess all folks get a little crazy once in a while.

"I've been thinking about your problem with the capriole," Mac went on. "I've got an idea."

"What?" Linda said excitedly. "Oh, Mac, tell me. I've tried everything I know."

Mac scratched his head. "Well," he drawled, "seems to me you should be giving Amber some kind of signal she already knows. When you want her to take a fence, do you use any kind of voice command? How do you tell her what to do?"

Linda thought for a second. "I whistle!" she cried. "Every time we come to a jump now, I whistle. I guess I do it because she nearly missed a gully once when it was almost dark. Do you really think it would work here?"

"Only one way to find out," Mac said.

"I'll try it," Linda declared. She shook the lunge rope and clucked her tongue.

When Amber was cantering again, Linda put her tongue between her teeth and gave a loud whistle.

Amber threw Linda a confused look out of the corner of her eye, but she didn't leap into the air. She just kept cantering around in a circle.

Linda was disappointed. "She didn't get it."

"Try again," Mac said calmly.

Linda shook the lunge rope to get Amber up to speed, then tried again. Still, nothing happened.

Linda's shoulders slumped. She halted Amber, then turned to Mac. "It isn't working!" she cried. "I just can't get anything right today."

Mac gave her a long look. "Now, what kind of talk is that?" he asked.

Linda looked at her feet. "Sorry," she mumbled. "What should I do now?"

"Coil that rope," Mac directed her. "Then come on over to this railing and mount up."

Mystified, Linda did as she was told.

"Now take Amber over the salt lick a couple of times. And don't forget to whistle," Mac said.

"Oh, I get it," Linda said. "Mac, how come you're so much smarter than me?" She grinned.

"Well, I guess I've got a few years' experience on you," Mac said, grinning back.

Linda vaulted onto Amber's bare back, and the palomino loped across the corral. As they came up to the salt lick, Linda took a firmer hold of the coiled-up lunge rope. She whistled. Amber leapt cleanly over the white block, then veered to avoid the fence on the far side.

Linda rode back to where Mac stood. "One more time," she said. "Go, Amber!"

When they'd done the jump again, Linda slid off Amber's back and uncoiled the lunge rope. "Okay, horse, this is it," she said. She gave Amber a kiss on the nose. "You can do it."

After Amber had been cantering for a few seconds, Linda whistled. It worked like a charm! Amber sprang up. Her forelegs were tucked neatly beneath her as she sailed through the air. When she landed, Linda let out a whoop.

"It worked!" she shouted. "Mac, you're the greatest! How did you figure it out so fast?"

Mac shrugged. "Just logic," he said. "Now, I've got work to do." He sauntered away.

Linda kept Amber cantering. She tried the leap again. And then again. Each time she whistled, Amber rose into the air like a swallow. Finally, Linda brought her to a stop.

She threw her arms around Amber's neck. *"You're the greatest, too,"* she said.

She took Amber into the barn and rubbed her down with a soft cloth. Then she sent Amber out into the pasture to graze with the other horses. Nacho, the Shetland pony, whinnied with delight when he saw Amber.

"See you in a while, Amber," Linda called. She watched the golden mare greet Nacho. Then she turned and walked up to the house.

"Linda, come here a minute," Bronco called as Linda passed his study.

"I had a call from a lady named Susan Carson," Bronco said when Linda stuck her head in. "She asked my permission to use Amber in 'Diamond Street.'"

"Oh." Linda nodded. She'd forgotten all about "Diamond Street." Her high spirits dimmed rapidly.

"I told her if it was all right with you, it was all right with us. She sent me some papers to sign. The schedule says Amber should be on location tomorrow at eight-thirty A.M. sharp. All right?"

"Okay, thanks." Linda heaved a sigh.

"Something wrong?" Her grandfather gave her a sharp look from under his bushy eyebrows.

"I don't know. I'll tell you about it later," Linda answered. She went into the den and dialed Kathy's number. She tapped her fingers nervously on the table as the phone rang.

Kathy answered. "Hi, Linda," she said in a neutral voice. "I can't talk long—we've got a lot of customers right now."

Linda wondered if that was true. The dinner rush didn't usually start for another hour or so. Would Kathy lie to her to get off the phone?

"Listen, Kathy, we have to talk," she began. "I'm sorry I acted so dumb this afternoon—I didn't mean to spoil the picnic."

"Oh, Linda, I know you didn't," Kathy said. She sounded relieved. "I was feeling just terrible about it all day."

"You were?" Linda felt a great weight lifting from her mind. "Then you don't think I was wrong about Joanna?"

"Huh? What are you talking about?" There was a sudden, wary note in Kathy's voice.

"About Joanna deciding that she doesn't like me," Linda said. "Isn't that what you're talking about, too?" she added hopefully.

"No, it's not." Kathy sounded annoyed. "*I* was talking about the way you were acting so weird all

61

afternoon. Listen, Linda, I don't know why you think Joanna's such a terrible person. She's not. She's really nice. She's just . . . well . . . different. You know. She's a Hollywood star."

"But Kath—" Linda shook her head in frustration. She took a deep breath.

"Kathy," she began again. "I'm not making this up. Didn't you notice the way Joanna ignored me all day? How she pretended I wasn't even there? And did you see the way she had Bob and Larry wrapped around her finger?"

"No, I didn't see any of that." Kathy sounded mad. "All I saw was you sulking around and acting all . . . all snooty. You want to know what I think? I think you're jealous because Joanna is a star and you aren't. You're jealous of all of us, as a matter of fact. You're mad because we all got parts on 'Diamond Street' and you didn't. And I think that stinks!" She banged down the phone.

Slowly, Linda replaced the receiver. She sat down on the edge of the den's comfortable old sofa. Her stomach felt as if it were filled with lead.

"Honey?" Linda looked up. Bronco was standing in the doorway. "What's the matter?" he asked gently.

"Oh, Bronco!" Linda jumped up and ran over to hug him.

"There, there." Bronco stroked her hair. "Now, what's wrong? You can tell your grandpa."

Linda swallowed hard to keep from crying. "I think I just lost my best friend!"

6

Bronco sat Linda down on the couch. "What do you mean, you've lost your best friend?" he repeated.

The story of the day's events came pouring out. Tears pricked Linda's eyes as she told her grandfather about the morning casting session, and the picnic, and the way Kathy had just yelled at her.

"Oh, now, Linda, I'm sure it can't be all that serious," Bronco said when she'd finished. "You and Kathy have been best friends for a long time. It sounds as if she's a little star struck, that's all. She'll get over it."

"Do you really think so?" Linda asked. "You don't think she's right? You don't think I'm just making things up because . . . because I'm mad that I didn't get a part?"

"Well." Bronco smiled down at his granddaughter. "Don't you think there might be a little—just a *little*—bit of truth in that?"

Linda sat up straight. "I didn't make up Joanna being mean to me. I swear I didn't!"

"I know. But maybe you're making it a little easier for Joanna to pick on you, honey. Maybe you're feeling sorry for yourself. And people who feel sorry for themselves aren't much fun to be around."

Linda swallowed, then nodded. It was hard to admit, but Bronco was right.

Outside, the dinner bell rang, calling the hands in to the bunkhouse. The family usually ate at the same time.

Bronco rose. "I don't mean this Joanna Curtiss isn't behaving like a spoiled brat," he added. He looked Linda in the eyes. "But you shouldn't let her get to you."

Taking a deep breath, Linda smiled at her grandfather. "I see what you mean. Thanks, Bronco."

The next morning dawned bright and clear. Linda was in the barn by six-thirty, feeding and grooming Amber.

"Today's your big day, Amber," she said as she

vigorously scrubbed the mare's withers with the currycomb. "Hollywood is going to fall in love with you."

Amber snorted and bit off a wisp of hay from the net in her stall.

"I know—you're not going to let it go to your head, are you?" Linda asked. She put down the currycomb and reached for a soft body brush. She swept Amber's sides with long, smooth strokes, brushing away tiny particles of dried mud. For a few moments she worked in silence. Then an idea struck her.

"Hey, maybe there'll be a chance for you to show everyone your capriole," Linda suggested excitedly. She picked up a metal-toothed comb and attacked Amber's mane. "Wouldn't that be neat? I bet you'd steal the show. No one would even notice Joanna Curtiss." She grinned at the thought.

"'Morning, Linda," called one of the hands as he passed by. "Oversleep today?" He smiled.

Linda laughed. Six-thirty must really seem late to the ranch workers—they were usually up by five, and out on the range by six.

"I guess you overslept yourself, huh?" she called. "It must be lunchtime for you guys."

"Guess you're right," he answered. "Say, I hear your palomino's going to be featured in this TV show they're making over in Lockwood."

"That's right," Linda said proudly. She moved around to comb out Amber's tail. "I'm fixing her up for it right now."

The hand gave her the thumbs-up sign. "Best of luck to you both." He left the barn.

Linda combed Amber's tail until each hair shone. Then she went over Amber's legs with the body brush, paying special attention to the silky feathering over the mare's pasterns and fetlocks.

Finally, Linda grasped Amber's white forelock and combed it. Amber rubbed her head against Linda's shoulder, neighing softly with pleasure. "I love you, too," Linda told her.

Linda saddled Amber up. But instead of putting on the bridle, she just untied the lead line and led Amber outside. "No offense," she said, "but I'm riding Rusty today. I want you to be fresh as a daisy when we get to the shoot."

Going back into the barn, Linda saddled Rusty, a chestnut mare who was one of the ranch's brood horses. She led Rusty out and mounted up.

Amber let out a disconsolate squeal. "Oh, it's no

big deal," Linda scolded her. "It's only for a day or two." But she admitted to herself that it sure did feel strange to be riding a horse other than Amber.

It was just seven-thirty. Linda glanced at the ranch house. Luisa was outside, tossing corn to the chickens. She looked up, saw Linda, and waved. "Have fun," she shouted.

Linda waved back. She took a deep breath, as butterflies started to dance in her stomach. It was time to face Kathy, and Joanna, and everyone else who was included in the cast of "Diamond Street." Well, nothing is going to ruin my day today, she told herself.

"Let's go," she cried, winding Amber's lead rope around her hand. Then they were off.

Not wanting to tire Amber out, Linda took her time getting to the shoot location. But even so, she arrived on site early.

It was the same place where she'd knocked Andy Hatfield off his horse trying to "rescue" Joanna's stunt double. They were redoing that scene today. Nervously, Linda tethered the horses and went over to check in with the stunt director, Mr. Steiner.

Linda's heart sank as she saw that "Mr. Steiner" was actually Lou, the man who'd yelled at her that first day. He was sitting in a folding cloth chair next to a big camper, marking off lines in a black binder.

"Excuse me," Linda said. "I've brought Joanna's new horse."

Lou glanced up. When he saw Linda, he groaned. "Not you! Of all the horses in this town, Joanna had to pick yours?"

"Hey, Lou, take it easy. Why don't you have another five cups of coffee?" a woman's voice said. "You sound a little grouchy."

Linda turned and saw Joanna's stunt double standing behind her. "Hi," the woman said with a friendly grin. "I'm Joy Workman."

"I'm Linda Craig," Linda replied.

Joy took Linda's arm and led her away. "Don't mind Lou. He's really a pushover," she advised. "You know, that was some nice riding you did the other day. I saw the way you sent Andy flying. Ever consider doing stunt work?"

"Not really," Linda confessed.

"Maybe you're a little too young to be thinking about careers just yet," Joy conceded. "But if you're still riding in ten years, come to Hollywood and look me up. You'd be a big hit!"

Linda glowed with pleasure. "Thanks," she said.

"But, you know, I couldn't have done it without Amber. She's my horse—you'll be riding her today, I guess."

"The palomino? Great. Can I go meet her?" Joy asked.

"Sure. Come on." Linda grinned at Joy. She already liked the stuntwoman a lot. Something about Joy made her feel very comfortable.

"Amber, Joy. Joy, Amber." Linda made it a formal introduction.

"Pleased to meet you," Joy said gravely. Then she broke into a smile. She dug into her jeans pocket and produced a piece of carrot. "Okay if I give her this?"

Linda nodded and Joy fed Amber the carrot. "Aren't you a beauty," she said softly as Amber nuzzled her palm.

Joy turned back to Linda. "To tell you the truth, riding really isn't my specialty," she said. "Oh, I've trained some, but leaping out of burning buildings or crashing cars is more my kind of thing. But I look like Joanna, and I guess my riding's good enough. Still, anything you can tell me about Amber would be a help."

"She's really easy to ride," Linda assured Joy. "She practically reads my mind sometimes. I barely even touch her neck with the reins, and she does a sharp turn, right to where I want her to go. And you never have to use a crop with her, or anything like that. All you have to do is tell her to go, and she'll run faster than . . . than a speeding bullet!"

"That fast, huh?" Joy cocked an eyebrow at Linda. "Pretty high praise."

Linda blushed a little. "Okay, maybe I'm exaggerating," she said with a laugh. "But Amber really is smart, and she really is fast. You'll see."

"Attention, people!" Lou's voice suddenly boomed out. Linda turned, startled. He was standing on the tailgate of the jeep, shouting into a battery-powered megaphone.

"All right, people, we need to take some light readings. Stand-ins! Places, please."

"What's a stand-in?" Linda asked Joy.

"Someone who stands in the star's place to make sure all the camera angles are right, and the lighting is adequate, and stuff like that," Joy answered. "In this case, me—I stand in for Joanna. Not everybody uses one, but if you knew Joanna Curtiss, you'd know that she can't be bothered with all that waiting around. She's probably not even here yet."

Linda smiled sympathetically.

"Gotta go," Joy said to Linda. "I'll talk to you later." She walked over to Lou.

Just then Linda caught sight of Bob, on Rocket. He rode up to her and dismounted.

"Hi," Linda said. They hadn't really talked since the picnic yesterday. She wondered if Bob was still mad about how she'd behaved.

"Hi," he said. There was a silence.

"Listen, Bob, I'm sorry—" Linda began.

"I want to say I'm sorry—" Bob began at the same time.

They looked at each other and burst out laughing. "Okay, you go first," Bob said.

Linda looked at the toes of her boots. "I'm sorry I was such a baby yesterday," she said. "I know I was acting stupid." She looked up. "Okay, your turn."

Bob's ears turned red. "I'm sorry, too," he mumbled. "Bronco gave me a talking-to last night. I guess I didn't see how Joanna was picking on you. And it wasn't fair of us to leave you out the way we did. If I do it again, you can . . . well, you can kick me."

"Really? And you won't kick me back?" Linda asked. "Is that a promise?"

"Just this once. After that, look out!" Bob growled. But he was grinning broadly.

72

"All right! Amber's my witness."

"Sorry, but I need the witness for a stand-in," came Joy's breathless voice. She ran up and untied Amber's lead rope, then led the mare over to the jeep.

"Wow, is that a stuntwoman?" Bob asked. He stared admiringly after Joy. "I'd love to be a stunt rider. Do you know her?"

"Uh-huh. She's really neat. If you're nice to me, maybe I'll introduce you," Linda teased.

Another jeep roared up to the site and stopped in a cloud of dust. The door opened, and Joanna Curtiss climbed out.

Joanna came right up to Bob. She didn't even look at Linda. "Hi," she said. "What are you doing here?"

"Linda and I came to watch," Bob answered. He glanced at Linda, looking a little nervous.

"Oh." Joanna's smile slipped a little. "I just wanted to tell you that Friday's my fourteenth birthday. I'm having a big party. Will you come?"

"Uh . . . well, I . . . let me ask my grandparents," Bob said. He looked very uncomfortable.

Joanna shrugged. "Sure, if you need their permission." She turned to go, then stopped. "Oh, and bring Larry, too. I want all my friends to be there."

"Phew!" Bob said as Joanna walked away. "I

guess now I know what you were talking about yesterday. She acted like you weren't even here."

Linda nodded. "And she didn't invite me to her party. I just don't get it," she murmured unhappily. "What did I ever do to her to make her hate me?"

Bob shook his head. "Beats me."

"Okay, places, everyone. This is scene five, take one. Quiet on the set!" Lou yelled into the megaphone. "This will be a take. I repeat, this will be a take."

Bob ground-tied Rocket. Then he and Linda sat on the ground by a clump of mesquite to watch the take. Linda could see Joanna sitting in Lou's director's chair by the refreshment table. She looked bored.

"Ready, Joy? Andy?" Lou asked. They nodded. "All right, cameras rolling? Everything set? *Action!*" Lou screamed.

Joy and Andy took off across the mesa. The jeep zoomed alongside Joy. One of the cameramen leaned out the window to get a close-up of Amber. She stretched out her neck and ran for all she was worth.

"Oh, look, Bob," Linda whispered. "Isn't Amber just great?"

"Cut!" Lou yelled. Joy and Andy reined in and circled back to him, looking puzzled.

74

A Star in the Saddle

"What was wrong with the take?" Joy asked.

"What was wrong with it?" the stunt director sputtered. "I'll tell you what was wrong with it. You were going too fast, that's what! What is this, a racehorse? Can't you slow it down? Andy hasn't got a chance of catching you—where's the suspense, huh? Now, let's do it again. And let's get it right!"

"There's your answer," Bob whispered to Linda. "I'd say Amber is *too* good." He grinned.

Linda chuckled. "Poor Joy. I hope she doesn't have to do this too many times."

Luckily, Joy was able to keep Amber in check on the second take. Linda could see that it wasn't easy for Amber. She didn't like the other horse chasing her so closely, but she did seem to sense what Joy wanted her to do anyway.

"Good work," Lou admitted. "I think that's a wrap. Let's just do it one more time, for insurance. This time I want you to start behind that rise there." He pointed. "Let's get up some steam *before* we start shooting."

"Hey, that was easy! I knew Amber would do just fine," Linda whispered.

Joy and Andy took their places on the far side of the rise. "And . . . *action!*" Lou screamed.

Joy came over the ridge first. Linda gasped and rose to her feet as she saw Amber barreling down the slope.

"Joy's sitting all wrong!" she cried. "She can't lean that far forward going downhill!"

It was too late. Even as Linda said the words, Joy tried to turn Amber to the right. Amber missed a stride. Joy pitched forward onto Amber's neck.

Then, as Linda stared in horror, both Joy and Amber went tumbling to the ground!

7 ••••

"No!" Linda cried. She raced over to where they had fallen. Oh, please, let Amber be all right, she prayed. And Joy, too—please let them both be all right.

As Linda skidded to a stop on the slope, Amber rolled over. Snorting and shaking her head, she struggled to her feet.

"Oh, Amber, thank goodness you're all right." Linda felt tears of relief wet her cheeks. She threw her arms around Amber's neck.

Joy's training had paid off. She had managed to pull her feet out of the stirrups and do a shoulder roll as Amber fell. But as she sat up a couple of yards away, she looked dazed.

"Joy!" Linda hurried over to her. "Are you okay?"

Joy squinted at her and gave a shaky grin. "Nothing broken, I think." She tapped her head with her

77

fingers. "But my brain is rattling around in my skull a bit."

"She needs a doctor!" Lou came puffing up the slope. Bob was right behind him. "Somebody bring a stretcher. Hop to it—let's go!"

The stunt director looked genuinely worried as he knelt by Joy.

"How are you, kid?" he asked anxiously. "Think you're going to make it?"

Joy nodded. "I've felt worse."

She tried to stand up, but Lou wouldn't let her. "That was a nasty fall. I'm sending you to the doctor—and no back talk!"

With a wan smile, Joy looked at Linda. "How's Amber?"

Linda ran her hands quickly down Amber's legs, feeling for tenderness. The golden mare didn't flinch. Linda heaved a sigh of relief. No breaks or sprains.

"I think she'll be fine," she said.

Lou scowled at Linda. "Why is it that every time I see you, I see trouble?" he demanded. "What happened? This horse is too green!"

"That's not true!" Linda cried indignantly. "She was doing fine!" She broke off, not wanting to say anything against Joy.

78

"Linda's right, Lou," Joy said. "It was my fault we fell. My balance was way off."

Linda looked gratefully at Joy.

Lou's scowl lightened a little. "Well, we got the take, anyway," he muttered.

Two men ran up with a stretcher and lifted Joy onto it. They carried her to the jeep and sped away toward Lockwood.

"Let's take a break, people!" Lou called. He turned to Linda and Bob. "Now what am I going to do?" he asked. "I had three more scenes with Joy today. Even if there's nothing wrong with her, they might keep her in the hospital overnight. My schedule is shot."

"Maybe Linda could fill in for her," Bob suggested.

Lou snorted. "Are you kidding? She's not union— and she's not old enough. It's against the law."

"I really am sorry, Mr. Steiner," Linda said. "Can't you do some other scenes today?"

"Maybe. I have to make some calls." Lou stomped off to the camper.

Linda picked up Amber's reins. "Come on, girl, let's see you walk," she said coaxingly. She and Bob led the mare slowly back to the site.

As they approached, Linda caught sight of Kathy.

She was standing with her hand on Patches's reins, talking to Joanna.

Kathy looked up and spotted Linda and Bob. For a second, she looked as if she were going to say hello. But then she seemed to change her mind. She gave Linda an expressionless stare instead.

Linda sighed. It felt just awful to be in a fight with her best friend.

"Excuse me, miss." A tall man with thick black hair came up to Linda and put his hand on Amber's bridle. "My name's Tim Hong. I'm a veterinarian. Mr. Steiner's orders—I've got to make sure this horse is fit before we proceed."

"Where are you taking her?" Linda asked.

Tim Hong pointed behind the camper. A couple of other horses were grazing there. "That's our setup," he explained. "We'll rub her down and let her graze a while. It looks like there's going to be a delay in the schedule."

"Okay," Linda said. "Can I visit her?"

"Sure." Tim Hong gave her shoulder a friendly squeeze and led Amber away.

"Wow, it's almost noon," Bob said, looking at his watch. "I've got to go meet Larry at his house. Want to come along?" he asked. "We're going for a ride in the desert."

Linda gave Bob a smile. She knew he was trying to be extra nice to her. But she didn't really feel like going with him.

"No, thanks," she said. "I think I'll hang around here a while longer."

"Okay, see you." Bob ran over to where he'd left Rocket. He swung into the saddle and galloped off. Linda watched him forlornly as he went.

She felt at loose ends. Kathy wasn't talking to her, Bob and Larry weren't around, and Amber was with the vet.

I guess I'll ride over to Amy and Marni's and see what they're doing, Linda decided. She picked up Rusty's reins and looked at the chestnut mare. "Ready for a little exercise?" she asked.

Rusty gave her a disgusted look and blew out a loud sigh.

"I feel like that, too," Linda told her. She put her left foot in the stirrup and swung up. "Well, let's go for a nice gallop. Maybe it'll cheer us up."

As soon as they cleared the filming site, Linda clapped her heels to Rusty's sides. "Hyaaah!" she cried.

Rusty broke into a leisurely jog.

"Oh, come on, horse. You can do better than that," Linda scolded. She prodded Rusty again.

Reluctantly the chestnut mare began to lope.

"You remind me of Patches," Linda told her. "And don't take that as a compliment."

For the next couple of minutes, it was all Linda could do to keep Rusty to a lolloping canter. Every time she stopped squeezing the mare with her knees, Rusty would slow down.

Finally, Linda had had enough of Rusty's jolting footsteps and her laboring breath. She reined the mare in to a slow jog.

"Rusty, I like you," she said. "But you're not Amber. Not by a long shot."

They reached the Browns' driveway and turned in. Once again, Kelly's horse, Cinder, was tied to the porch railing. Linda dismounted, tossed Rusty's reins over the rail, too, and knocked on the kitchen door.

Marni answered it. "Hi, Linda," she said. "Come on in. We're all upstairs in my room. Amy can't decide what to wear in our scene tomorrow."

"What to wear!" Linda exclaimed as she followed Marni up the stairs. "But isn't it an enormous crowd scene?"

"Uh-huh." Marni rolled her eyes. "No one's going to see us, but try telling *her* that. She's already gone through her entire closet. Now she's working on mine."

Linda laughed. "Well, you never know who might be watching."

They went into Marni's room. Clothes were everywhere—on the floor, on the bed, tossed over Marni's desk and desk chair. Kelly was at the closet, pulling out more. Amy was standing in the middle of the room in a checked button-down shirt and blue jeans. Her red hair was pulled back into a French braid.

"Hi! Linda, you got here just in time. What do you think of this outfit?"

"Amy, you look just like you look every day," Linda said, puzzled. "It took you this entire mess to find that?"

"You don't like it!" Amy wailed.

"Oh, no, here we go again." Kelly flopped down on the blouse-strewn bed with an anguished sigh. "See what you did, Linda?"

"No, Amy, it looks really great," Linda said quickly. She held in a laugh.

"Where's Kathy?" Marni asked Linda.

"At the shoot," Linda told them. She felt a little uncomfortable, wondering if Kathy had told any of them about the fight.

"I haven't seen her at all since she got that speaking part," Kelly commented. "Is she rehearsing all the time?"

"Not really," Linda mumbled. "I haven't seen her much, either, but I think she's been spending a lot of time with Joanna Curtiss."

"Joanna Curtiss? They're *friends?*" Amy shrieked. "Why didn't she tell us?"

"Wow!" Marni added. "What are we waiting for? Let's go over there now!"

"Not me, you guys," Linda said, shaking her head. "I just came from there. Doesn't anyone want to go for a ride?"

"I'll go with you," Kelly volunteered. "I'm getting a little tired of all this stargazing."

"Well, we're not!" Amy declared. "Come on."

The four girls clattered downstairs and out the kitchen door.

"How come you're not riding Amber?" Marni wanted to know. Linda told her about the accident and the vet.

"How exciting! It sounds like 'Diamond Street' is definitely the place to be," Amy said. "See you guys later."

"So long." Linda and Kelly mounted their horses and trotted out to the main road.

"Where should we go?" Kelly asked.

"I don't know—anywhere, as long as it's away from the shoot. Nobody talks about anything else anymore. I'm getting sick of it," Linda confessed.

"I guess you must be pretty upset that you didn't get to be an extra," Kelly said, giving Linda a sympathetic glance.

"At first I was. But now it's all the other stuff that's really bothering me." They passed the gas station and headed west.

"Stuff like what?" Kelly asked.

As they rode, Linda told Kelly about Joanna and Kathy.

"And now Kathy's really mad at me. She thinks I'm jealous of Joanna because she's a star," Linda said ruefully.

"Tough luck," Kelly murmured. They rode on in silence.

They reached a fork in the trail. If they took the right fork, Linda knew, they'd end up at the spot where she and the others had picnicked the day before. She winced and guided Rusty to the left.

"You know something?" Linda kicked Rusty into a reluctant lope. Kelly and Cinder pulled up alongside.

"What?" asked Kelly.

Linda frowned. "I was thinking . . . maybe Joanna

doesn't have too many friends back in Hollywood. Maybe that's why she's acting this way. Maybe she doesn't know how to make friends. She only understands kids who are impressed with her glamorous stories." She sighed. "But I can't tell Kathy that. She won't even talk to me."

Kelly shook her head. "Or maybe Joanna Curtiss is just plain spoiled," she suggested. "If I were you, I'd— Hey! Look at that!" She pointed.

The girls had reached the foothills of the mountains. In front of them, a wisp of gray cloud was drifting down the side of a ridge.

Linda sniffed, then started to cough as a tendril of cloud brushed by her face.

"That's smoke!" she gasped.

Kelly looked at Linda. Her blue eyes were wide and fearful. "Do you think the fire is getting closer?" she asked.

Linda took a firmer grip on the reins. "We've got to find out," she said, trying to sound brave. But her heart was pounding double time.

She dug her heels sharply into Rusty's flanks. Rusty neighed and began lolloping toward the ridge where the smoke had been.

Kelly and Cinder were right behind Linda as she pulled Rusty to a halt atop the ridge. Both girls stared down at the scene that stretched before them.

The whole valley was blanketed with dense gray smoke. It rolled up and over the rimrock to the north. At the crest of the next ridge, Linda could see tongues of flame shooting up to lick the sky. Black streamers of soot hung in the air, and the smell and heat of the forest fire was everywhere.

"Linda!" Kelly's voice was little more than a squeak. "Look at it."

"I see." Linda spoke loudly to keep her voice from shaking. She felt Rusty shudder with fear and laid a calming hand on the mare's neck. Now, more than ever, she wished she was riding Amber.

"What should we do?" Kelly asked.

Linda wheeled Rusty. "Come on," she said. "The fire's coming our way. We've got to warn the town before it's too late!"

8 ◆◆◆◆

Linda kicked Rusty. "Let's go, horse," she shouted.

For once Rusty needed no encouragement. Like all horses, she feared fire. She galloped down the slope toward town as if she were being chased by a horde of wasps. Kelly and Cinder pounded along beside them.

"Is the fire really serious?" Kelly called. Her voice pulsed with the beat of Cinder's hooves.

With one hand, Linda pushed her hat down more firmly on her head. "I don't know," she shouted back. "Bronco says the rangers track the fires pretty closely. But this one looks as if it's getting out of hand."

Kelly nodded.

The girls rode without speaking for a few moments. The only sounds were the drumming of their horses' hooves, the creaking of their saddles, the jingle of their metal bits, and Rusty's harsh breathing. And, through it all, they heard the distant roar of the flames.

They flashed past the turnoff to the picnic spot. Linda glanced down the trail. It ran beside a stream that looked cool and inviting. But Linda knew that if the fire had already reached the rimrock, the picnic spot would be surrounded by flames. The thought made her shiver.

"Come on, Rusty," she urged the chestnut mare. "We've got to go faster!"

Rusty's head was beginning to droop, and there were flecks of foam on her muzzle. But at the sound of Linda's voice, she stretched out her neck and poured on a fresh burst of speed.

"Good girl!" Linda cried. "I take back everything I said earlier. You're a great horse!"

"Think she'll make it all the way back to town?" Kelly asked anxiously.

Linda nodded. "She'll make it. We're more than halfway there now." She crouched low over Rusty's withers, and they pounded gamely on.

The girls reached the gas station about ten minutes later. They reined in to a jog. Rusty's sides were heaving, and sweat darkened her neck and flanks. Even Cinder, who was a tough, wiry mustang, looked exhausted. His breath rasped in his throat with every step.

Linda and Kelly jogged up Main Street to the sheriff's office. They ran inside, barely stopping to tie their horses to the porch rail. Linda raced past the astounded desk deputy and threw open Sheriff Garcia's office door.

"Sheriff Garcia!" Linda cried. "The fire! It's heading our way!"

"You've got to call the rangers!" Kelly put in. "If they don't stop it, it'll eat up Lockwood."

Sheriff Garcia was a tall, thin man with dark hair. He looked up from his work and whisked off his reading glasses.

"What?" he demanded. "Are you young ladies sure of your facts?"

Linda nodded, breathless.

"We just came from the foothills," Kelly declared. "They're all on fire—we saw it!"

The deputy appeared beside Kelly. "I-I'm sorry, sir," he stammered. "They just ran right over me—"

Sheriff Garcia waved the deputy to silence. "Never mind that!" he barked. "Get the ranger station on the phone. Those men have to be alerted right away."

"Yes, sir." The deputy scurried back to his desk.

"Now," the sheriff said, turning back to the girls. "Tell me exactly what you saw."

Linda and Kelly did so. "And the smoke was all the way to the rimrock," Linda finished up. A horrifying thought struck her. "Oh, no—if the fire gets into the woods this side of the mountains, it'll put Rancho del Sol in danger!"

The sheriff shook his head. "Deputy Hodgkins is talking to the rangers right now," he said reassuringly. "You can be sure they'll take care of it. They've been extra busy these last couple of days. The fire's been bad—we've had a lot of wind shifts. Now they've been alerted, thanks to you." He gave Linda and Kelly a little bow. "They'll get this sector under control fast.

"I'll tell you what you can do, though," Sheriff Garcia continued.

"What?" Linda and Kelly asked together.

"Give Hodgkins a hand rounding up the volunteer fire fighters. He's got only one phone, and it could take him a while to track people down. If you would each take a list, you could double-check that everyone's been alerted. I'd appreciate it no end."

"Sure thing, Sheriff," Linda said.

"Just give us our lists," Kelly added.

The sheriff directed Deputy Hodgkins to divide up the list. Linda made the deputy promise to call Rancho del Sol first, to alert Bronco and Doña to the possible danger. Then she and Kelly hurried back outside.

Poor Rusty looked exhausted. Linda decided to cover her list on foot. "I'll be back for you as soon as I'm done," she promised the mare. "I'll take you over to the Browns' and give you a nice rubdown."

Most of the men on Linda's list worked in town. There was Mr. Akers from the Express office; Mr. Jefferson from the pharmacy; Paul and Colin Reardon, who ran a novelty store; Mr. Spencer, Larry's father, who owned the Lockwood saddlery; and a few others. Linda's heart sank as she came to the end of the list. It was so short! Would there be enough men to beat back the fire?

Just then the sputtering noise of a helicopter came faintly to Linda's ears. She looked up. There were five choppers in the sky, heading west, toward the fire. All five had the red forest ranger's emblem on their bottoms.

"All *right!*" Linda yelled. She took off her hat and waved it joyfully in the air. The rangers were on the job.

Grinning, Linda headed for the Express office, her

first stop. It was still important to round up the volunteer fire fighters, she knew. But now that the rangers were here, everything would be all right. She could feel it!

It was only three o'clock, but Amy and Marni's mother was home from work early. When Linda appeared with Rusty, she was happy to let Linda stable Rusty temporarily in their barn. She made lunch while Linda rubbed down Rusty. Then she offered to drive Linda back to the shoot.

"Thanks, Mrs. Brown. I really appreciate this," Linda said as she climbed into the Browns' pickup truck.

"Well, it's the least I can do, after you've worn yourself and Rusty out alerting the rest of us about this fire," Mrs. Brown answered. A worried frown creased her brow as she started the truck. "Anyway, I want to find Amy and Marni and get them home. I don't like them being out when there's a wildfire nearby."

They drove toward the site. "I wonder if they're still shooting," Linda mused. "It must be pretty smoky out there. They're right in the path of the wind."

"If the director has any sense, he'll realize it's time to pack up," Mrs. Brown said. She smoothed a few red hairs out of her face, frowning. "I hope so, anyway," she murmured.

"Here's where you should turn off." Linda pointed at a track of matted grass. "The site's just over that ridge."

As they bumped over the ground, Linda leaned out the window, trying to see what was going on. After a moment, she pulled her head back in.

"I don't know," she said doubtfully. "It doesn't look like they're filming anything, but it doesn't look like they're packing up, either."

"We'll see about that," Mrs. Brown said in a determined voice. She parked the truck and they climbed out.

Smoke hung heavy in the air. It made Linda cough. But the site was teeming with activity. Crew members were running around, frantically checking equipment. A couple of angry-looking men in business suits were talking to Susan Carson. Lou Steiner was shouting into his megaphone, his face red with annoyance.

"Afternoon shots are canceled," he announced. "Come back tomorrow, people. And don't complain to me. I have enough problems!"

At that moment Linda caught sight of Amy and Marni. The red-haired sisters were hard to miss. They were standing by the camper, talking excitedly with Kathy. Linda gulped.

Marni turned and caught sight of her mother. "Mom, what are *you* doing here?" she demanded. "Oh, I'm so embarrassed!"

"Come on, girls, time to go home," Mrs. Brown said calmly.

"Oh, Mom! Did you have to come out here in person?" Marni spoke in an anguished whisper. "I mean, we have our horses. We can get home fine by ourselves. You don't see anyone else's *mother* here, do you?"

"Yeah, we're not babies," Amy put in.

"All right, grown-up young ladies," Mrs. Brown said with a smile. "You can ride your horses, or you can come in the truck with me, but I want you home. *Now.*"

"Okay, okay," Marni grumbled.

"See you later, you guys," Amy said to Linda and Kathy.

"So long," Linda said.

"So long," Kathy echoed.

"You two should get on home, too," Mrs. Brown said. "Linda, will you be all right? Do you have a way to get home?"

"I'll be fine," Linda assured her. "Amber's here. I'll ride."

"All right, then. Give my best to your grandparents. And Kathy, tell your mom I'll call her tonight. So long." Mrs. Brown went back to her truck and drove off.

There was an awkward silence. Then Linda cleared her throat. "Well, I guess I'll see you later, too, Kathy," she said uncertainly.

"Wait a second, Linda!" Kathy burst out.

Linda looked at Kathy, surprised. Kathy hung her head.

"I just wanted to tell you . . . well, I know you were right about . . . about Joanna," she said in a whisper. "I'm sorry I didn't believe you before."

This sounded serious. "What happened, Kathy?" Linda asked sympathetically.

"We were talking this morning, and Joanna said something really mean." Kathy paused.

"Something mean about whom?" Linda asked.

"About you," Kathy said with a sigh.

Linda set her chin. "What did she say?"

Kathy sighed again. "We were talking about her birthday party. She said she wasn't inviting you because you were trying to steal her part on 'Diamond Street' from her."

Linda's jaw dropped. "Huh? Where'd she get that idea?"

"That's what *I* asked her," Kathy confided. "She said you broke up the shoot that first day on purpose. She said all you wanted was to get attention and show off your riding. I told her she was wrong, and then she got mad at me and said a whole bunch of mean things. Linda, she made Ms. Carson not give you a part, and she pulled that stunt yesterday to get everyone on her side, and a bunch of other stuff." Kathy shook her head. "And now she's ticked off at me, too."

Linda didn't know what to say. "I'm sorry," she murmured. She waved a wisp of smoke out of her eyes.

"Well, I'm not," Kathy declared. "If that's what the glamorous Joanna Curtiss is really like, Hollywood can have her!

"That is, if she gets back in one piece," Kathy added, her eyes twinkling with mischief. "I did start thinking of all sorts of mean tricks to play on *her*. Like putting glue on her saddle, maybe."

Linda giggled. "Oh, don't! Poor Amber would be stuck with her forever!"

"You're right. That would be totally mean to Amber," Kathy agreed. "Well, then, how about one of those big lizards, like the one Larry and Bob had yesterday? We could put it in Joanna's bed."

Linda looked at Kathy. "Poor lizard!"

Kathy started to laugh, and Linda laughed with her. It felt good to be friends again!

The sudden roar of a helicopter reminded Linda that it was time to leave the open range. "I'm going to get Amber," she told Kathy. "Want to come over to my house? Luisa's making tacos for dinner."

"Okay," Kathy agreed. "But I'd better call my mom and dad as soon as I get there. They'll be worried about me."

Linda nodded and walked around to the back of the camper, where Tim Hong had told her Amber would be.

But there were no horses there!

A wave of fear swept over Linda. She ran around to the camper door, knocked, and threw it open.

A young woman in a green jumpsuit was sitting inside. "Tim left half an hour ago," she said in response to Linda's question. "All the horses got picked up by their owners when we first heard about the fire. Tim didn't have any reason to stick around."

"But that's impossible!" Linda cried. "One of those horses was mine—Amber, the palomino. And I never picked her up. Where is she?"

"I don't know," the young woman said. "Hey, Adam!" She waved to a guy with curly brown hair who was lugging some equipment past the camper door. "Did you see that palomino horse around here recently?"

Adam scratched his head. "Palomino—is that the gold-colored horse?"

"Yes!" Linda was nearly dancing with impatience.

"Yeah, I think I did see that horse," Adam answered. "Couldn't miss it, as a matter of fact. Her royal highness was having trouble staying on its back."

"You mean Joanna Curtiss?" Linda asked faintly. She was beginning to get really scared.

"Yup."

"Which way did they go?" Linda asked.

Adam thought for a second. "Let's see. Joanna was in an awful snit about something. I think they went that way." He pointed.

"Oh, no!" Linda moaned. Adam was pointing west, toward the rimrock—and right toward the heart of the forest fire!

9 ••••

"How could Joanna be so dumb?" Linda cried. She ran out of the camper, leaving Adam and the young woman in the green jumpsuit staring after her.

Linda raced up to Kathy and grabbed her arm. "Joanna and Amber are in big trouble," she said tensely. "Joanna rode Amber toward our picnic spot."

Kathy gasped. "The fire!"

Linda nodded grimly. "It's already at the rimrock. If she keeps going along that trail, she and Amber will be caught in the smoke. Joanna won't be able to find her way out—and I doubt she has enough sense to let Amber have her head. We've got to rescue them."

"H-how?" Kathy quavered.

Linda looked around. Nearly everybody had packed up and left by now.

"You take Patches and get the sheriff," she said, thinking rapidly. "I'm going to ask Mr. Steiner to take me in the jeep to find them."

"But, Linda, that's so dangerous," Kathy protested. "What would Bronco and Doña say?"

"I've got to do it, Kathy," Linda said fiercely. "If someone doesn't get to Joanna now, we may never see her—or Amber—again." She swallowed hard, fighting back tears at the thought.

Kathy nodded. "Okay, I'm on my way." Her brown eyes were dark with worry as she looked at her friend. "Please be careful, Linda."

"Don't worry about me," Linda told her with a shaky smile. She ran over to Lou Steiner.

The stunt director was just climbing into the jeep with Andy Hatfield when Linda tugged on his sleeve. "Excuse me, Mr. Steiner," she said breathlessly.

"I smell trouble," Lou announced, scowling. "All right, what is it?"

Linda flushed. "It's Joanna Curtiss," she said, wishing Lou were a little less gruff. "She's missing—and she's riding my horse."

"How do you know?" Lou snapped.

Linda told him what Adam had told her, including the fact that Joanna had been seen heading straight for the fire.

Lou's face darkened. He smacked his fist into his palm. "Why wasn't someone with her? How could this have happened? I'll tell you, that girl is more trouble—" he muttered. Then he spread his hands. "Well, what can I do about it?"

Andy Hatfield stuck his head out the window. "Lou, what are we waiting for? Let's get back to town."

"Please, Mr. Steiner, we have to do *something!*" Linda burst out. "They'll get lost in the smoke. Joanna doesn't know the land around here. Please, can't we drive there in the jeep? I know the way—I'll show you. We can't just leave them alone in the fire."

Lou heaved a deep sigh. "I knew you were going to say something like that," he growled. "And you know what makes it even worse? You're right."

"I—I am?" Linda asked, astounded. She hadn't expected him to agree so quickly.

"Yes, you are, and thank you very much for giving me indigestion," Lou said with a grimace. "This is all I need—chasing after little girls on horses. I thought my stunt days were over." He opened the door to the jeep. "All right, we're going for a scenic tour. Well, what are you waiting for? Come on, get in."

Linda recovered from her shock and scrambled

into the front seat. She wedged herself beside Andy Hatfield, who grinned at her.

"Well, if it isn't my old friend Calamity Jane," he rumbled. "Life's never dull with you around, is it?"

Linda smiled back at him. "I guess not," she said. His large, easygoing presence was comforting.

"Spare me," Lou groaned and started up the jeep. They were off.

The jeep rattled over the flat ground. Linda craned her neck to see how the fire was spreading. The smoke rolling over the mountains was so dense she couldn't tell what was happening.

In the driver's seat, Lou mopped at his streaming eyes. "I'm allergic to smoke," he moaned. "I tell you, if we get out of this alive I'm going to apply for a job in the mail room. This movie business is too much. Too much!"

"Take a right by that stand of ponderosa pines," Linda directed. "That's where the trail forks, see?"

Lou nodded miserably. "Just barely. I'll probably crash this thing."

"Want me to drive?" Andy offered, but Lou grunted and shook his head.

Two white-tailed deer bounded past the jeep, heading in the direction of Lockwood. "Guess they're going to check in at the hotel tonight," Andy said with a chuckle.

Linda smiled in spite of her worry.

They drove on, and in a few minutes came to the tree line. Linda spotted one of the orange trail markers that signaled the southwestern edge of Rancho del Sol. She leaned forward and peered out the driver's side window. The picnic trail would be coming up any minute.

"There's the trail we want," Linda announced as it came into view. She felt her stomach knot up. If only they weren't too late already! Oh, Amber, she said silently, please be all right.

Lou turned the wheel, and they bumped onto the narrow trail to the picnic spot. They had to go very slowly, since the way was little more than a bridle path. Linda could hear the roar of the fire plainly now, and the hot, gusting wind that blew in the open windows was full of ash. She stifled a cough.

Andy let out a long whistle. "We're a bunch of crazy fools, driving into this," he said in a thoughtful voice.

"Wait! Stop the car!" Linda cried suddenly. They had come to the clearing by the stream.

Lou stepped on the brake, and Linda sprang out of the jeep. She ran over and looked at the soft ground by the edge of the water. "There are Cap's hoof-prints, from when he reared yesterday," she said aloud.

Lou stepped up and looked over her shoulder. "So?" he said.

"And these are Amber's prints. See the little dent in her shoe?" Linda asked, pointing. "That's an identification mark, so that when I see her hoofprints I'll always recognize them."

"What is this, cowboys and Indians?" Lou grumbled. "How is this going to help us find that brat?"

Linda was concentrating so hard she barely heard him. "And here are Amber's prints again!" she said excitedly. "We didn't ride this close to the water yesterday, so these must be from today."

She looked up. "Mr. Steiner, they were here! The question is, where did they . . ."

Linda's voice trailed off as she saw where the hoofprints led—to the water's edge. Joanna and Amber had forded the stream.

"Oh, no," Linda whispered. "This is trouble."

"What? What?" demanded Lou.

"Is there a problem?" Andy asked, coming up beside them.

Linda sat back on her heels. There certainly was. Joanna had forded a stream that swung up into the hills again. She might have thought she was getting away from the fire by crossing the water. But in reality . . .

"Joanna and Amber are trapped on the wrong side of the stream," Linda said in a flat voice. She felt as though a fist had just closed around her heart.

"What do you mean? How do you know where they went?" Lou demanded.

Wordlessly, Linda pointed to the opposite bank. Amber's prints were clearly pressed into the mud. They turned north, running along the edge of the stream.

Linda lifted her gaze. The air in front of her was shimmering with a heat haze. Through the trees she could see the first tongues of flame licking toward the stream. In a few more minutes, the fire would reach this very ford!

"Can we follow them?" Andy asked.

Linda thought about it for a second. "Maybe we can," she replied, jumping to her feet. "Joanna's probably figured out that she went the wrong way. So the logical thing for her to do now is to try and stay ahead of the fire by going *north*. If she's being logical about it," she added doubtfully.

Lou snorted. "I wouldn't count on it."

"Well, anyway," Linda went on, trying not to let

that get her down, "she did go north at first. So let's say she's still heading that way." She beckoned to the two men to follow her. "We'd better get moving. I'll explain as we go."

Lou threw a dubious look at the jeep, but it was clear that the big vehicle couldn't get through the dense growth along the stream bank. He reached in to grab the first-aid kit and megaphone.

"Just in case," he murmured to Andy. Then both men hurried after Linda.

"Joanna's probably looking for another ford. The problem is, there aren't any for a long way. The stream widens and gets a lot deeper about a quarter mile up from here. Also, it's a cutaway—it makes a gorge through the hills. The bank is about fifteen feet above the water—kind of a little cliff."

"So what are you saying?" Lou asked.

Linda bit her lip. "I guess I'm saying it's going to be pretty hard for them to cross back over," she admitted. Tears welled up in her eyes. "But we've got to find them and at least try to get them back!"

"Hey, take it easy, kid. We'll bring them back," Andy said. He patted Linda's shoulder.

His words didn't bring Linda much comfort. Oh, Amber, she thought miserably, if anything happens to you I don't know what I'll do!

They hurried on in silence. It was a nightmare journey. By now, the smoke was making everybody's eyes stream, and the hot ashy air was parching their throats. Once a flaming piece of debris landed on Linda's hand. It made a painful blister before she brushed it off.

And every time Linda looked across the stream, the flames had edged a little closer.

After they'd been going for about twenty minutes, Lou called a halt.

"Look, I'm not a quitter," he said in a gruff voice. Linda could tell he was trying to be kind. "But I don't think there's much we can do here. And if we don't get back to the jeep soon, there might not *be* any jeep for us to get back to."

Linda gave him an anguished look.

The stunt director threw up his hands. "All right, fine, forget I ever said it," he grumbled. He strode ahead of Linda and Andy. "Let's keep going. Maybe we'll get lucky and reach Alaska before the fire catches up with us." But he didn't sound genuinely angry.

They stumbled on. Linda felt despair creeping over her. In spite of the fire's fierce heat, she shivered.

Then a high, faint noise came through the crackling of the flames. Linda looked up, suddenly alert.

"What was that?" she asked hoarsely.

"What was what?" Andy responded.

"Listen! Didn't you hear a noise?" Linda demanded. "Wait—there it is again!"

This time, it was unmistakable. Amber's neigh!

Linda let out a joyful whoop, which turned into a coughing fit. When it subsided, she cried, "They're there! We found them. *Amber!*"

She peered through the smoke at the opposite bank. Yes, now she could see Joanna and Amber!

They were at the edge of a bluff that overhung the stream at a height of about twelve feet. A half circle of flames towered behind them. Amber was prancing sideways, her ears flat back against her head. Joanna didn't seem to be even trying to control her.

"I know Amber—she's terrified," Linda told Andy and Lou. If we don't get her out of there now, she's going to spook completely."

Lou held the megaphone to his mouth. "Joanna! It's Lou Steiner. Can you hear me?" he shouted.

"Yes," came Joanna's answer. They could hardly make the words out through the roar of the flames. "Help!"

"Joanna, you've got to get the horse to jump over that bluff," Andy shouted. "Can you do it?"

"I don't know how!" Joanna wailed.

Lou and Andy both looked at Linda. "You're the expert," Lou told her. "What do we do now?"

Linda's heart was hammering so loudly in her ears that she could barely think. What could she do? Amber understood her hand signals and knee pressures, but now Amber was yards and yards away from her. Only a voice command would work.

A voice command. "That's it!" Linda said. "Please, please let this work!"

Linda took the megaphone from Lou and shouted, "Joanna, kick Amber. Kick her hard!" She put her fingers to her lips.

Just as Joanna punched Amber's flanks with her heels, Linda let out the loudest, most piercing whistle she had ever given. "Up, Amber!" she yelled. "Up, girl!"

Amber surged forward. Then, at the edge of the bluff, she soared up and out, floating through the air like a falling leaf.

It was a perfect capriole as Amber extended her back legs gracefully behind her. She hit the deep water below with a tremendous splash.

"Hooray!" Linda cheered wildly. She jumped up and down on the bank.

A Star in the Saddle

Lou and Andy were grinning broadly. "All *right*," Andy kept saying. "All *right*."

"You did good, kid," Lou told Linda. But she wasn't even listening. She was up to her knees in the stream, grabbing Amber's bridle. Joyfully, she pulled the golden mare and her rider out of the water, up the near bank and to safety.

10 ◆◆◆◆

Once they were safely on the bank, Linda threw her arms around Amber's neck and buried her face in the horse's mane. Tears streamed down her cheeks, and they weren't all from the smoke.

"Oh, Amber, I'm so glad you're back," she whispered. "I was so scared."

Amber snorted and rubbed her velvety muzzle against Linda's sleeve.

A spark flew into Linda's hair and smoldered for a second before it went out. Linda didn't care. Amber was safe, Joanna was safe, and that was all that mattered.

Joanna slid shakily off Amber's back. She seemed dazed. She stared at Linda for a second, as if she were about to say something. Then suddenly her knees buckled. Andy stepped forward and caught her as she fell.

"You've had quite an adventure, huh?" he said with a grin. Joanna nodded weakly.

"All right, people, break up the party. Let's get back to the jeep," Lou ordered.

"You're right!" Andy exclaimed. Linda gave an emphatic nod, too. Their situation was still urgent.

"Can you walk?" Lou asked Joanna.

She shuddered. "I hope so. But it's going to be a long time before I get into a saddle again!"

Linda hid a grin. That would be fine with her. She suspected it would be fine with a lot of horses, too.

Linda took Amber's reins, and the group made its way back along the stream bank as quickly as they could. Still, the trek took a good fifteen minutes.

Finally, they emerged from the trees into the clearing where the jeep was parked. Linda cried out, alarmed. The fire had reached the trees on the west side! A tall fir was burning fiercely. Just as they reached the jeep, the tree split apart with a crack. A section of flaming trunk hit the ground twenty feet away.

Amber squealed in terror and tried to rear. Joanna shrank away from her. Linda hung on to the bridle and calmed the frightened horse. "Easy, girl," she crooned. "We're going now."

Amber's eyes rolled wildly. She was close to panic, Linda could see. Something had to be done.

"Andy—your bandanna," she gasped.

Andy nodded and handed her his red kerchief. Quickly she made a blindfold for Amber. Linda knew that once Amber couldn't see the flames anymore, she'd be easier to handle.

"Okay," she said briskly. "Let's get out of here."

Lou, Joanna, and Andy jumped into the jeep. Linda climbed onto the running board on the passenger's side. Still holding Amber's bridle, she signaled Lou to drive on.

With Amber trotting obediently behind the jeep, they headed back the way they had come.

A sizable crowd was waiting for them back at the film site. Sheriff Garcia was making an announcement, trying to keep everyone calm.

Kathy, Bob, and Larry were huddled together, whispering. Bronco was pacing back and forth. Doña was leaning against a jeep, looking worried to death.

As soon as Doña saw Linda, she rushed forward and pulled her into a huge hug. "Thank goodness you're safe!" Doña said, her voice catching.

"How'd you know I was here?" Linda asked, astonished.

"Kathy called us and told us what you were doing," Doña answered.

Linda flashed Kathy a grateful smile. Kathy smiled back and gave her the thumbs-up sign.

Bronco hugged Linda, too. "You gave us quite a scare, young lady," he said. "But we're awfully proud of you."

"I wasn't very brave," Linda mumbled into his shirt. "I was scared the whole time."

"That's when bravery counts the most," Doña said with a gentle smile. Then she added, "But please, don't *ever* do anything like that again."

"Especially not when *I'm* in the neighborhood," Lou's voice boomed. He and Andy stepped over to the group. "Ahem"—he looked slightly embarrassed—"No, seriously, I'd just like to tell you people that your granddaughter really saved the day. If she hadn't pushed Andy and me into searching the woods, there could have been a major tragedy. We're all grateful to her."

"Hear, hear," Andy cheered.

"I promise I won't do it again, Doña, unless I have to," Linda said. She felt very solemn. "I just couldn't leave Amber and Joanna to wander out there all alone."

"No, you couldn't," Bronco agreed. "Next time, though, ask Sheriff Garcia to help you out."

Linda looked over at the sheriff. "Did all the fire fighters show up?" she asked him. "Are they getting the fire under control?"

"Yes, indeed," Sheriff Garcia said, nodding. "It'll take some time, of course, but the rangers' latest reports say they'll have little trouble containing the blaze. I don't think you folks need to worry—they'll dig trenches and stop it before it gets even as far as the western edge of Rancho del Sol."

"That's great," Linda said.

"All right!" Bob chimed in. "Bronco and Doña, can I help dig trenches?"

Doña looked severe. "Young man, don't you ever give up?" she asked Bob.

"Nope," he answered with a mischievous grin.

Everybody laughed. Then Bronco and Doña started talking to Sheriff Garcia about the fire-fighting effort. Linda walked back to the jeep and Amber.

When she got there, she was surprised to see Joanna Curtiss still sitting in the backseat. Joanna climbed out and faced Linda. She looked very unsure of herself all of a sudden.

"Um, I just wanted to say . . . well, I guess I want to thank you for helping get me out of that mess." Joanna looked off at a point somewhere beyond Linda's head. "I mean, after all the stuff I did to you."

Linda gave Joanna a long look. "Why did you do those things? Why did you decide you didn't like me?"

Joanna scuffed at the dirt with her boot. "It wasn't really that," she said in a small voice. "I never hated you or anything. I guess I was kind of jealous of you, that's all."

"You? Jealous of *me?* Why?" Linda asked incredulously.

"I don't know." Joanna shrugged. "Because you have everything going for you—you're a great rider, you have lots of friends. You don't have to make yourself different—people just *like* you. You do everything right."

"But you're a famous actress!" Linda protested. She draped an arm over Amber's neck. "You've got tons of fans who think you're just great. You must be doing something right, too."

Joanna thought about that for a second. Then she smiled at Linda, a genuine smile, for the first time.

"Yeah, maybe you're right," she said.

"Excuse me! Attention, people," Lou said, clapping his hands for silence.

"On behalf of the cast and crew of 'Diamond Street,'" he said when everyone was quiet, "I'd like to invite all of you to dinner at the Huntington tonight. There will be a guest of honor." He bowed to Linda.

"Me?" Linda gasped. She could feel herself blushing.

"In fact, there would be two guests of honor," Lou went on, "if the Huntington allowed horses inside." His eyes were twinkling. "But since that's out of the question, I guess I'll just have to talk contracts with Amber in the stables."

"Contracts?" Linda asked, puzzled.

"Listen, kid, with the jumping trick you pulled today, you two could be the hottest new team in Hollywood. How about it?"

Linda laughed. "I don't think I'm cut out for a glamorous life," she said with a look at Joanna. Joanna grinned back at her.

Lou sighed. "Oh, well, it was a thought. Come on, people, let's get back to the hotel and rest up." He beckoned to Andy and Joanna.

"Hey, Mr. Steiner, if you're looking for stunt riders, my friend Larry and I have a few moves that'll knock your socks off," Bob called eagerly.

Lou turned and looked at Bob. "Yeah? All right, let's talk over dinner." He climbed into the jeep and drove away.

"Yeah!" Bob crowed. He and Larry slapped each other's palms.

Linda and Kathy looked at each other and made identical faces of disgust. Then they both burst out laughing.

Doña shook her head. "Well, I'd like to get home and wash off some of this grime. Linda, you are an absolute sight. If you could see your face—it's covered with soot."

"Let's go," Bronco agreed. "Larry, Kathy, want to join us?"

"Thanks, we will," they said in unison.

Linda sighed with happiness as she climbed into Amber's saddle. Everything had worked out perfectly after all. Amber and Joanna were safe, she and Kathy were friends again, and everything was back to normal. On top of it all, she and Amber had been "discovered" by Hollywood!

"Life is pretty exciting, huh, Amber?" she murmured to the golden mare.

Amber tossed her head and gave a ringing neigh.

"I guess that's a yes," Linda said with a laugh. She shook the reins. "Come on. Let's go home!"